MIDNIGHT APOCALYPSE

VIOLA TEMPEST

Midnight Apocalypse
© Copyright 2022 Viola Tempest

All rights reserved. No part of this publication may be reproduced,
distributed, or transmitted in any form or by any means, including
photocopying, recording, or other electronic or mechanical methods,
without the prior written permission of the publisher, except in the case
of brief quotations embodied in critical reviews and certain other non-
commercial uses permitted by copyright law.

Any references to historical events, real people, or real places are used
fictitiously. Names, characters, and places are products of the author's
imagination.

Cover Design by CReya-tive

CONTENTS

MIDNIGHT APOCALYPSE

VIOLA TEMPEST

"The Pyramid has ruined my life," Freya Moore sighed, moving her phone from one ear to the other.

"What are you trying to say?" a feminine voice on the other end of the phone call replied. It was hollow and distant, as if she might not have been quite as interested in the answer.

"Juliet, you know how much my parents' relationship has been affected by all of this. It's impossible to get rid of this disease," Freya attempted to explain to Juliet, her best friend from the past eight years.

It pained her to discuss it, but if she could somehow gain Juliet's interest in the subject, along with a modicum of understanding, it'd be worth it.

"It made my dad cheat on my mom with another woman, You don't think that's bad enough? And instead of making it work, they..."

She trailed off, and there was a pregnant pause. The silence across the atmosphere felt oppressive enough to touch.

"Your mom hooked up with someone else?" Juliet interjected, finishing Freya's sentence, but turning it into a question.

"Love her for that," Freya said sarcastically and rolled her eyes. "And to top things off, my brother got hooked on drugs and became depressed. He was already struggling, but that just broke him. He felt so helpless, and now, I've seen him on that app more and more often, too."

"Yeah, I feel terrible for Cyrus." Juliet now sounded genuinely sympathetic.

As if Cyrus' plight, in some way, trumped her parents'. Another moment of silence made the sound of the inevitable digital hum of the cell phones so much clearer. Freya felt compelled to ask if her friend was still on the line when Juliet cut in again.

"So, did you get the intern position at the Pyramid?" she asked. "That could change things, and also give you some purpose."

"I don't know, haven't checked my mail yet. If I get it, then it will be the perfect birthday present." She smiled to herself. *The best gift is the one you give to yourself*, she thought. "I hope I get it. I really need to bring the Pyramid down,"

Freya continued, her smile vanishing when she pronounced the name of the social media platform.

Suddenly, a knock fell upon the door of her room.

"Freya, can we talk?" Her mother's voice sounded anxious. The way it always sounded these days. "Also, some mail came for you."

"Jules, I'll talk to you later," Freya said, and once her friend said goodbye, she turned off her cell.

She carelessly tossed the old thing onto her bed; it bounced against the pink fluffy duvet cover and slowly slid to the carpeted floor. Freya stood still for a moment and contemplated the perfectly engineered piece of technology as it laid facing up. The screen was dark, like one giant lifeless eye staring up at the ceiling, where a huge poster of her favorite band had once hung. Ancient residue from all the tape was still clearly visible. A distant memory of her rebellious youth, when the images of tattooed men with long hair and nose rings stood as a sharp contrast to the pink door that separated her childhood room from the rest of the house.

Freya squinted at the phone and clicked her tongue. As if she were expecting it to call out to her. Begging for her to pick it up. To unlock the untold treasures and promises that the digital world had to offer. She smirked and tapped the doorknob a couple of times before she decided on what to do next.

Do I really need my phone for this? she thought. *Let's see what life has in store for me instead. Maybe something that I've been wanting for the past few months.*

With determination, she grabbed the worn brass colored doorknob — it, too, a jarring contrast to the cheery pink door, and exited.

"Is everything okay, Mom?" Freya asked as she strode

through the kitchen and grabbed her mail from the island in the center of the room.

It'd been weird to call her that at first, she still remembered. It'd actually taken her a few years to go from Mr. and Mrs. Moore to Mom and Dad, but in the end, it had been worth it. The first day Freya had called the Moores their parents, their eyes lined up with tears, and their smiles were the biggest she'd ever seen. Jumping from foster home to foster home ever since she had memories, life had been hard, but when she finally landed with the Moores, she knew she was home. It had just been harder to admit it out loud after so many failures.

Her mother smiled sadly. "Yes, I think so..."

She could sense the hesitation in her mother's already contemplative voice. It made Freya do a double take, having decided to ignore her at first and proceed with her own business. The apparent emotion in the voice made her question if her mother had done something out of the ordinary. There was a sound of guilt hanging in the air of the stark white kitchen with its dark marble countertops.

Her mother tapped the countertop of the island in an anxious rhythm. Her jagged, broken fingernails created an odd beat as they struck the crafted marble. Freya looked at her with a raised eyebrow, waiting with bated breath for the words to come.

"You see... I... um...," her mother stammered.

Her eyes darted erratically from side to side in an unfocused manner. As if she'd expected something to appear and stop her from delivering the message.

"Your dad is getting married." She finally sighed.

For a moment, Freya couldn't quite fathom what her mother had said, as if the words coming out of her mouth hadn't made sense. A mess of guttural sounds without real meaning, but when she observed her mother, the realization dawned on her. The way her eyes gradually became used to the dark. The words began to step out of the distortion, coming into focus and making sense.

She looked away, at her mother's fingers still tapping against the white swirling patterns on the dark, polished stone, and then up at her face. Her blue eyes were wet with tears; they reflected the LED lights of the spots placed in neat rows on the ceiling. The pain was evident in them as her lower lip trembled.

"What?" Freya felt a pang of the shock reverberate through her body. The news made her muscles twitch as she tried to regain control of her body. "He's remarrying?" She turned away from the situation, moved toward the sink, and turned on the faucet. "Damn, he really is something. It hasn't even been a month since your divorce, and he's getting married again?"

She put her hand under the running water before realizing that she wasn't holding a glass. The Pyramid had ruined the only good thing she'd found in her life, making things worse each minute, and she didn't know what to do.

"Yeah, well, he called last night and wanted his children to know about it." Her mother moved toward her with a glass. "I know, you want me to be strong." Her voice was cracking, but she tried to stay in control. "But Freya, I'm just extremely tired of feeling rejected."

"I know, Mom." Freya took the glass and put a hand on her mother's arm. "I know. I just don't get how he thought this was an appropriate time to do this."

Freya could hear the anger in her own voice. How it trembled ever so slightly. She wanted to scream the words, but then thought better of it. Who would it help at this point? She might feel better. Like her body releasing the pressure of intense hatred, but what good would it do to spit venom over her douche of a father to his former wife? Shouting at the choir, it would be.

She then realized the water was still running, and she quickly swept the glass under the tap, and then went over to hug her mom's fragile body. Her tiny frame felt bony as Freya wrapped her arms around it, trying hard to not spill the water down her back. It was as if all the tragic events recently had worn her down, turned her into a shell of her former self.

She let go of the hug and handed her mother the glass of water.

"Drink up, Mom," she said. "It'll calm your nerves."

Her mother did as she was told, and then placed the glass on the island. That was when Freya noticed that it was one of the promotional *Dawn of the Dead* glasses her father had brought home from Burger King years ago. Painted yellow eyes looked back at her from their perch on the island counter. She always hated that movie, but still loved the image imprinted on the glass in bright colors. Now, like the memory of her father, they seemed dull and tarnished.

Freya grabbed a soft pack of Newport and tapped the top on her hand until a cigarette emerged like a rabbit from its burrow. She handed it to her mother, then went for the mail.

Among the slim envelopes with tiny plastic windows — obviously containing offers for free credit cards and insurance proposals — she found the one she had eagerly waited for. A standard white envelope, with the Pyramid logo clearly visible.

She turned it over and broke the seal in order to slip out the letter, and began to read the words in clean crisp font.

Congratulations, you have been selected as an intern. Your superiors will decide your permanent employment after a period of time...

Something like that. It felt less important what the actual wording was. The important part was what the gist of it meant.

She smiled. It was done.

"Mom," she said and searched for a lighter. "The Pyramid accepted me as an intern, according to the letter. I start on Monday."

Her mother smiled through bloodshot eyes while fishing for a lighter with trembling hands.

"That's amazing, sweetie, so proud of you," she replied hesitantly and lit the cigarette, then proceeded to hold out the bright flame toward Freya.

Freya looked at her mother as she inhaled the fresh smoke from the newly lit cigarette. The once proud person who used to be the archetype of the perfect, ideal parent, now reduced to a husk, a shadow of a real person. One incapable of caring for herself. Her pain was so clear in everything she did, the way her eyes were never quite dry from the tears she shed daily, the way she would stop in the middle of every task she performed. Confusion surrounded her like a wet blanket thrown over her shoulders, not comforting or warm, instead oppressive and weighted, like the thoughts that sent her spiraling deeper into the abyss.

There had been a time when this woman would do anything for her children so they could have a perfect and healthy life. So, they were cared for, clean and proper. It seemed like another life, another time. Seeing her like this, the victim of drastic changes, made Freya sick to her stomach. This was a person she no longer knew.

Her parents had divorced over a month ago, and since then, her mother had brought several strangers into her bed. Men she had met over various dating apps and then, without vetting them properly, taken home. It made Freya's head spin. Her mother acted like a teenager, experimenting with random strangers, while her father was getting married for the second time.

This was not the future she had envisioned, but she knew where it stemmed from. She often blamed herself for leaving, for taking that trip to Istanbul and making their parents doubt themselves. She had received a call from Cyrus while she was there and had to rush home as fast as possible, hoping the cheating was only something in Cyrus' head, and not something real. But when she returned, her life had been turned upside down. She still remembered the moment Cyrus had said the dreaded words as it'd been yesterday, "I think they might divorce."

Everything in her life had been beautiful before the Pyramid, she could see that now, even though she could never get back those perfect mornings. Life would never go back to normal. But she couldn't blame herself; the Pyramid was the one to blame.

Monday is going to change the direction of my life, Freya thought as she looked at her own reflection in the kitchen window, looking out over the busy street outside.

She watched the figure looking back at her, mechanically moving the cigarette from her fingers to her lips. A gaunt, pale looking figure with sunken eyes stared back at her. The LED lights overhead made her appear hollow, like the stylized zombie figurine sitting still on the counter. A shadow of her. One that only showed the negative aspects of her. Not the strong and vengeful woman she truly was.

You have to make sure you stay strong, she told the reflection, and it winked back at her.

CHAPTER TWO

"I loved my home," Kairi Harridan mumbled softly to her reflection in the window. Her visage looked back at her through the fog of dirt and grime. *I did, right? Or was it merely the peace and tranquility it offered me?*

Her steel gray eyes stared back at her, seemingly peering through her with cold and emotionless sharpness. Like two daggers made from tempered steel, unbreakable. The reflection refused to answer her, mostly because there were no answers to give. The home, those four walls that had surrounded her like a protective barrier, keeping all manner of evil out... It was a safe haven, but that might be all it was. She tried to picture it, but only standard stock photo images appeared in her mind.

She turned and walked down the hallway, her brown nightgown flowing behind her in a majestic fashion, like the perfect portrayal of a lady in a Victorian tale. Even though she had everything a mundane could desire, she still felt lonely in her mansion on the hill. There were servants at her beck and call at all times, but still, no one to relax her empty soul.

The grand hallway she strode down effortlessly reminded her of this fact. Empty eyes stared down at her from large portraits. They smiled at her, but not a single one of them meant the inanimate facial expression. Instead, it became a mocking leer from dead people she didn't know.

It was almost midnight as she lied down to sleep on her oversized bed, but she couldn't find any sleep. She stared at the heavy drapes, pulled tightly around her, that kept the outside at bay, watched as the wind stirred them slightly. Just as she kept the dark of night out, it refused to find her, like the two were separated from one another by the fabric, for sleep remained elusive. The fact tensed her soul; the harder she attempted to sleep, shutting her eyes tighter and tighter, the more vivid the visions and memories became.

The memories of how she had wronged others for her own pleasure. The images dizzied her mind and made her want to scream in hopes that it would release the anxiety built up inside. She gasped instead, not finding the strength to let her lungs expel the emotion, to have it leave her sick body. She needed to get away from it all and isolate somewhere far away. Maybe one day, she would find the tranquility her unconsciousness desperately sought, but at this moment, it was too late; her ambitions had shaken the world in chaos. She stood at a point of no return.

Her attempt at allowing her soul to escape her body was interrupted by a soft knock on her bedroom door. Kairi blinked a couple of times, listened intently to make sure she had heard it right. When the tentative knock came again, this time so softly that it was barely audible, she swung her legs over the side of the mattress, allowing them to appear through the drapes. The cold made the tiny hairs stand on end. She twisted her black hair into a sloppy makeshift braid over her left shoulder, and then, with trepidation, placed her bare feet on the weathered hardwood floor in order to see who had graced her with their presence at this time.

A petite woman with red hair stood at the other side of the heavy door and entered the room with a tray in her hands.

"Miss, you have a telegram," the woman said, bewildered at bothering her mistress this late at night. "And someone named Henry is waiting for you downstairs."

"Oh, you mean Henry Cooper, Silvia?" Kairi asked as she held out her hand to grab the telegram.

"Yes, miss," Silvia replied and stared dead ahead without emotion. "He says there is an urgent matter to discuss."

There always is, Kairi thought, but flashed a smile at the woman, who didn't seem to pay attention.

"Alright, I'm coming," she said, tapping the telegram on the side of the tray.

She looked back at her comfortable bed, then made

her way toward the large walk-in closet on the other side of the room.

"Have you ever wondered what it would feel like to slow down time?" she asked as she rifled through her wardrobe. "To the extent that particles moved with the sheerest delicacy, the sound of pounding hearts dissolved in bliss, and the urge of irresistible violence mutated?"

She found the appropriate evening gown and slipped into it while Silvia arranged her shoes.

"I don't know, miss," Silvia replied and picked up a brush for Kairi's hair. "Maybe there are good ways to achieve the same goals, more positive ways."

Kairi stayed silent, considering the thought. Silvia had a tendency to give non-answers, but she couldn't quite figure out if this was one or not. If the mousy little creature had really understood what Kairi was saying and replied with an intelligent statement. She had nothing else to say.

Once Silvia was finished, Kairi rose to observe her dress, a black number with some length to it in the back. She slung a white shawl over her shoulders and turned to see how it all came together. Maybe a bit overdressed for Henry Cooper, but if there was anything Kairi knew better than anybody else, it was how to make an impression.

———

THERE IS ART BEHIND EVERY ACTION; NOTHING IS A result from nothing. There is always something that leads to another. This was how the human world came into existence, from nothingness to endlessness. The drive to evolve this world came from the human idea to better their reality. They made utensils, buildings, gadgets, and the fastest modes of communication. They improved education, traveled to space, and finally, went to the moon. With these leaps and bounds in progression, the world transited through various phases, from simple conflict to war, and in the end, to finding mutual common grounds. A common enemy to fight.

"You look beautiful, as always," Henry commented as Kairi walked down the large spiral staircase.

"Thank you, Henry," Kairi said with a sincere smile, careful to take each step with measured accuracy so as not to trip on her heels. "Navy blue really suits you."

Henry Copper was an average white man, with blonde hair and blue eyes that one might feel drawn into. Kairi would've described him as striking rather than every day handsome. Like a stock photo of a generic good-looking man in a frame purchased from Target.

She guided him into the grand parlor, and he let her take the lead as she showed him to one of the large baroque couches. Kairi took the seat across from him.

"Well, Ms. Kairi," Henry said, unbuttoning his jacket and leaning back on the couch. It elongated his body at an impossible angle. His red power tie hung limply down his torso. "I'm convinced you have heard all the recent adjustments our security team has made in screening the new algorithm," he appraised her with a knowing smile. "It has achieved the level of manipulation that you desired in the population," he continued when she didn't react to his words. "That's why I've brought you the recent reports." He passed on a large manila envelope to Kairi.

Silently, she went through the recent cases of destruction, and how the Pyramid was slowly numbing the mind of humans, incapacitating their abilities to think for themselves and make informed decisions.

"This is amazing, Henry," Kairi responded as she placed the open folder on the glass table between them. "Good work, but I'm sure there is another matter that you wish to discuss." Kairi eyed the man sitting with a relaxed attitude before her. "It makes no sense that you would deliver these files at this hour," she added, and then she leaned toward him, hands clasped together in a non-threatening way. "It could have waited until the morning."

"Indeed," Henry said and shifted uneasily in his seat. "There is something significant, and perhaps urgent, that I wish to discuss. There are some artifacts that we have discovered in the archives. I'm sure you're aware that we've been reorganizing them, and I've had a team work there for a few weeks now. We'd found a few other things of interest, but nothing major. This time, my team is fairly certain that we've found something of significant value... and with a history behind it. But in order to figure out if this is the case, we need your permission to access the forbidden files."

There was a brief silence as Kairi digested the revelation Henry laid before her. They had concealed and locked away everything that Cabal had retrieved over the years. How could some artifacts, pieces of history buried away behind barracks, have suddenly appeared in the company?

"Who found these artifacts?" Kairi raised her brow in an inquisitive fashion.

It wasn't the first time that some of Cabal's artifacts were found in their possession. Some of them had been concealed and hidden, others long forgotten, but it was known for them to be found every now and again. Some of them didn't mean or matter much, but others... Others could change the course of the world.

"Well, um..." Henry began to hem and haw. "We're not

a hundred percent sure. Someone on the team left it on my desk, but they came in when I wasn't around, and even though I asked, I haven't found out who it was yet."

"Interesting. Can you have the artifacts delivered to my office by tomorrow morning?" Kairi asked as she relaxed her body and got ready to get up from her seat.

"Sure, Kairi."

"Perfect, thank you so much, Henry." Kairi rose from her seat, gesturing for Henry to do the same. "Walk with me for a bit."

Henry nodded and followed her out through the grand windows and onto the elaborate balcony that faced the busy suburban streets.

A few people walked up and down the streets, ignoring those around them, eyes glued to the screens before them.

"Look at that," Kairi said and held out her hand toward the mindless shadows of humans strolling aimlessly. "This is what we did when we rolled out the Pyramid."

"I am well aware," Henry replied and leaned against the stone railing. "Our team has done great work here. These people are completely ignoring everything that is going on around them. More interested in stopping and taking selfies."

A young mother with a stroller stopped in front of a poster, and then leaned over to take a picture of herself in front of it.

Kairi grinned. "You think they're mindless now? Just wait until the next phase begins."

Henry bit his lower lip at her words, watching her eyes turn dark with vengeance.

———

THE HISTORY AND ASSOCIATION BETWEEN CABAL AND the Pyramid ran deep. It came about around the beginning of civilization as an ancient corporation, although the word didn't exist yet. Throughout the years, they managed to work around various mediums to make society run the way they saw fit, and to fulfill their own vendetta.

At the beginning of time, the world ran based on prophecies, black magic, and other mystical beliefs that benefitted this mysterious and clandestine collaboration. Through academic evolution, their perspective of control changed, or to be more specific, their idea of how to best control the minds of the people, shifted. As an example, during the industrial revolution, they backed capitalism in the pursuit of keeping their pockets lined. During the postmodern era, they used social media as a mean to control a mechanism that, at first glance, appeared liberating, but instead, instilled rebellious ideologies.

Swiftly and inconspicuously, Cabal became the biggest corporation behind the Pyramid. They were not just aiding the usual militia or rebellion against society as a whole, but in fact, were an ominous entity that wanted to run the world. With heightened pride in being the most stable organization, their views did not intervene with the boundaries of society, yet still dominated everyone's ideologies. They used secrecy and privacy to slowly integrate the world. Their only goal... was world domination.

Just like the Illuminati, Cabal kept everything hidden and sacrificed the traitors, or whatever threats might come their way. They even got to the point of leading an army, owning a state, and becoming a political party. Still, every version of a cover they had found still gave away their true intent in one way or another. So, what the organization liked the most about the modern era was their ability to conceal themselves behind the web while running their businesses from an island only a few privileged members knew about. They also had their headquarters, hidden deep in the desert, where no one could find them.

The utter satisfaction to dominate every organization with one click progressed as the group grew. With time, Cabal found and began to pull the strings of the social media giant, the Pyramid. An engineered application set to strive for world peace, protect opinions, but instead, a rebellion rose. They found a way beyond laws, the army, racial discrimination, sexual restriction, and geographical outreach. A common ground that gave access to everyone.

The Pyramid.

———

THE ROOM WAS ALWAYS FULL WHEN THE SOCIAL AND internal affairs teams came together to read the devastating circumstantial shifts that people suffered at the hands of the Pyramid. There were bodies everywhere, and a constant mumbling of voices in the background. Like the backdrop of waves crashing against a cliff. People went over documents and reports, everyone with their own idea and opinion of what was transpiring and why.

Michael Knoll, the assistant manager of the social team, was a tiny clean-cut man with narrow shoulders and slim fingers. He looked like a person who had never done a day's grunt work in his life. His slim features made him cut the archetypical IT figure as he stood silhouetted against the large glass windows of the offices.

The assembled crowd of employees lowered their voices to a low murmur as Michael cleared his throat and looked at them. In his skinny hands, he held the latest report by Socio-wave, the leading social media magazine. It was a tradition he had started as soon as he assumed the position of assistant manager. He felt it kept his crew on their toes, and also kept the company in tune with various trends, as well as proof of their impact.

"Well," he started to say in his reedy voice that sounded like fingernails on a chalkboard — a reference that most of the employees were too young to understand. "It says here that the famous Pyramid health fitness model, Alain the Fitness Bunny, has gained immense popularity. This is due to her consciously being aware of her active lifestyle and constantly posting about it. What sets her apart from many of the other health influencers out there is that she earned a Masters in Nutrition, and she based her entire social media account around the importance of a healthy lifestyle. Not the first one to do so, but the first one to actively post about her own posting. Her feed is filled with practical workout routines, inspirational pictures of her clients' transformations, positive quotes, and Monday motivation. With several fantastic fitness programs, she has also worked as a trainer in the Fitness Freaks Gym upstate." Michael paused and waited for the inevitable next stage.

"As time went by," he continued as the team waited with bated breath. "She grabbed a lot of attention. Celebrities reached out to her, many TV shows casted her, the magazines posted articles about her achievements, and even universities invited her to give seminars on physical well-being. It's like living the perfect life in the modern era." He paused again and looked at the group, who were all intently waiting for the shoe to drop. "However," Michael continued after the appropriate amount of time had passed, "as time went by, her feed slowly changed. Her followers noticed that her confidence dropped. Her focus on nutrition decreased, and there were several videos posted of her binging on unhealthy snacks. In the end, she stopped monitoring her fats and carbs completely. This caused a great deal of concern among her followers, especially the most ardent and dedicated ones. They would comment on her posts and send her direct messages. On several occasions, they would send emails or personal letters in an attempt to reach out, but to no avail. In time, the posts just became worse and worse, more self-destructive and, in the end, Alain lost her charm. With that, the sole purpose of her Pyramid account was lost, too. Her interaction with followers, her family, friends, and loved ones simply stopped.

"This drastic change from being a social media sensation to a shadow of her former glory led people to assume that she must have experienced some form of heartbreak. That a partner had left her in abject misery. Some speculated that someone close to her had passed away, and surprisingly, based on her workouts and body portrayal, most believed that she started using steroids or drugs. However, it will forever stay a mystery as to what happened to her. How could a person lose herself so drastically?"

His voice cracked ever so slightly, quietly yet audibly, enough for others to notice. The murmuring became louder as the staff looked at each other with concern.

"Don't you think we've gone too far?" Dan Camper, the head manager of the social media team, rose from his seat and gave voice to what all those assembled were thinking.

"Well," Tara Styles, the senior data analyst in charge, cut in before Michael had a chance to reply. "Alain left the Pyramid, and no one really knows where she went after that. There has been no trace of her after she made her final post. She became a lost sensation, a social media mystery. We tried tracking her down through various channels, even contacted the authorities, but it feels like she just picked up and went completely off the grid."

"Yeah, I don't think anyone can find her now," Soha Rabir, an intern, rose from her seat and chimed in. "We have come too far to change our direction now."

The murmur died down, and people began fidgeting with an uneasiness only present in the truly guilty. Most of them looked at their hands because they agreed with her. The power of being controlled by social media had caused many people to lose their ability to generate independent thoughts. Just like how Alain lost her cause and replaced it with fame and greed. The negative shift in dreams and goals had caused a plague amongst the youth.

"Look at all the social outlets in the world today." Dan took the floor again. "They are filled with people who barely associate with one another."

There was a hint of disgust in his voice, and he eyed his colleagues with contempt.

"Well, this was *supposed* to happen." Soha had not taken her seat, but remained standing. "We sold individualism, and now, people prefer their own company, and with that, the ability to flaunt independence and a free lifestyle. We are simply doing what we've been told."

She addressed the crowd as her voice turned into more of a mumble toward the end.

"This is ridiculous!" Dan threw his hands in the air and left the room while shaking his head.

He balled his hands into fists. The palms were sweaty, and his mind constantly begged him to cry out all the distress and disgust he was feeling. That was not how things worked around here... One needed to be more innovative than that and play it cool. One needed to slowly pave a broken way through the muddled landscape of labyrinthine cubicles.

Dan's mind kept spinning, thinking about the way things were nowadays. About how people spent more time alone in their homes than out and about with their peers. Couples disengaged from each other rather than sorting out their issues, and the pure bond between parents and children simply unraveled until nothing bound them together but a thin thread.

The element of surprise and excitement had changed to normalcy. People focused on the result, the endgame, as they preferred greed and want over the process and joy of acquiring it. This created an excessive need for quick money, and in turn, created a want for "get rich quick" schemes. More and more impatient people became easy targets for elaborate pyramid schemes.

"Hey, Dan," a familiar voice came up behind him, taking him out of his mind. "You lost?"

Oh, Freya, he thought.

"Hi, Freya." He halted without turning around. "I'm not lost, just a little shaken."

He turned slowly to give her a proper greeting. They were at the end of the hall by the elevators, and it looked like Freya was waiting for it, so he stood to wait by her side. Truth is, he loved looking at her, and a few minutes trapped by her side would be delightful. That welcoming smile and the comfort she radiated had pulled him toward her since the minute she'd walked into the building for the first time. It hadn't been long, but he'd made sure to run into her as much as possible since then. As if he were the moon held in orbit around her. It was a powerful attraction on his part, but she gave him no indication if she felt the same. Maybe the work status between them changed things. She was an intern for the social team, and he was a higher-up employee; people might see something happening between them as a power move on his part. It caused him to hold off on what he really wanted to do.

"Why, what happened?" Freya asked as she extended her hand and carefully placed it on his arm.

"Nothing, really." He didn't want to trouble her with his issues. "I'm good, are you hungry? Do you want to grab a bite?" he asked without thinking. He shouldn't have, but he couldn't help it.

The ding indicating that the elevator had arrived at their floor sounded cheerful.

"I would love to," Freya said and smiled at him.

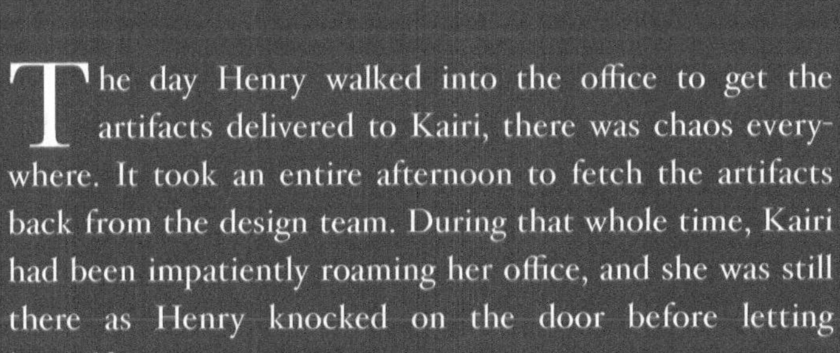

CHAPTER THREE

The day Henry walked into the office to get the artifacts delivered to Kairi, there was chaos every-where. It took an entire afternoon to fetch the artifacts back from the design team. During that whole time, Kairi had been impatiently roaming her office, and she was still there as Henry knocked on the door before letting himself in.

"Kairi, here are the artifacts." He handed over a perfectly closed case to her, as well as a small box.

As she opened the case, a golden glow illuminated the

room. The perfect circle surrounded Kairi like a halo and made her feel alive. She held the object in her hands with great care and slid her fingers across the surface.

"It's magnificent," she spoke with great awe in her voice. "Henry, on your way out, can you tell Kelly to call the archives from Cabal to send a man over? I need to know every single detail about this."

"Alright, anything else?" Henry asked as he looked at how Kairi had immersed herself fully into the artifact.

"No, thank you. You may leave," replied Kairi without even looking at him.

The other box could wait; she was smart enough to know that she couldn't handle two of those things at once. She already had a few artifacts hidden around that she was in the process of figuring out, but this one... This golden magnificent had to be different. She could feel it.

THE TEAM ARRIVED THE FOLLOWING DAY WITH ALL THE extracted files from the company archives. They held old piles of books and scrolls, and placed them on the table in the center of Kairi's office. The ancient, musty, papery smell spread throughout the room. At that moment, they felt that something evil had resurfaced., something that was supposed to be buried away. Kairi eyed the papers; she was afraid to open them, but the need for vengeance was too strong, and she needed to know. She had decided her path a long time ago, and now, she had to stay the course.

She held the first file that read: The War of Rusziye, 1881.

"According to the historians, this war shook the world," Clarissa Hamms, who was in charge of the archives, explained. "It changed the social structures, dynamics of the market. Educational sectors had an upheaval, but most significantly, people lost their minds. They went on this rampage of slaughter. There was a lot of bloodshed, a lot more than you can fathom. This insanity only enticed people to cross borders and kill others."

Clarissa was also a historian, the look almost stereotypical with the big round glasses that sat on the bridge of her nose. She was sitting across from Kairi, a look of utter concentration in her eyes.

"Where did this all begin?" Kairi asked.

"The north," Clarissa explained. "One day, out of nowhere, they started killing people, and it could never be put under control. Many think it was a plague that made them lose their minds. Slowly, the entire nation was wiped off the Earth, with only a few sane people left, who moved east."

"How did it stop?" Kairi asked in a low, raspy voice. She was afraid of the answer. No matter how vile her own ideas were, the thought of a full-on rampage shook her to her core.

"It never did... till now," Clarissa replied as she skipped through the pages. "Everything is just one click away. In fact, the people at that time tried their best to increase control, but with no success."

"They did find a way to control it, though," a male voice chimed into their conversation as he rose and spread out the fragile pages on the marbled floor of the office. "Look here, it says that they found a way to conceal the tremor that took away the north. Despite the numerous deaths, a scientist named Vaauztic from the Soviet Union made a device that trapped the devil. It is known as Scartzest."

"Keenan's right," Clarissa added, her eyes brightening, and she fell to her knees beside her second in charge. "They described the rampage as the 'devil' because no other force could have been capable of such heinous treachery against humanity. According to old scriptures, the devil wanted all humans dead."

"Do you think this device, this artifact, has confined the devil?" Keenan asked as he looked at Clarissa, then up at Kairi.

"Maybe. We need to find more archived sources to see if there is any evidence linking this device to the war," Clarissa said as she rose and started picking up her things.

"I think there definitely is. Otherwise, these files would not have been paired together with the files of the device," Kairi replied. "However, I couldn't find anything conclusive about it."

"Maybe it was supposed to be hidden away," Keenan muttered.

"Is there a problem, Keenan?" Kairi asked as she silently observed his movements.

"No, Kairi, none," Keenan replied.

"Well, good then," she said curtly. "Clarissa, can you dig deeper and find the files that are linked to this device? I don't want to waste more time; also, figure out how Cabal is involved in this process. And keep your mouths shut. I don't want anyone knowing anything about this."

She glared at Keenan, and then added, "Okay?"

He nodded.

Kairi watched her team saunter out of the office with their ancient scrolls and books before sitting down behind her desk, the artifact still glowing with its radiant light in front of her. She thought of the words Clarissa had said about rampage spreading around the world eons ago. It made her shudder. What had she uncovered? Was she ready to release yet another ancient plague upon the world? To witness so much death and destruction from her mansion on the hill?

The world? she thought.

What did she owe to it? A place that had never given her anything but heartache and pain. It had started when she was a child, alone and abused by a couple unfit to be parents. Leaving her for hours on end. They lived in a huge house, full of people and staff, that still felt empty at all times. Her father, the only one who had seemed to care about her, the only one to give her hope, left this world too early. Leaving her with an ungrateful, jealous, and competitive brother and a mother who wasn't one.

It became abundantly clear that this world was not for her. No one really wanted her. Kairi had always been an outcast from social groups at school, college, and even her neighborhood. People always looked at her weird, sideways, as if there were something wrong with her. The resentment and hate had grown inside her like a tumor. A disease filled with bile and malignancy, festering and bubbling, waiting to be released.

When she grew up, she studied media communications, psychology, and sociology in order to figure out the dynamics of the human mind, of how social constructs were made, and how to end them. Every turn of the page of textbooks reminded her of the name-calling, the food thrown at her in the cafeteria, the scorn and punches in the corridors. How teachers turned a blind eye while sipping their coffees in the lounge.

She had decided that if she was to be excluded from social settings, then those settings had to be destroyed.

This world doesn't belong to you, she thought and stared at the artifact. *It belongs to me.*

———

THE FOLLOWING DAY, NEWS BROKE OUT ABOUT WHAT had happened to the famous scientologist, Roland Brook. He was an active member of the Church of Scientology and gained popularity relatively early on in life with his healthy life choices. The normality of his routine was followed by over ten thousand followers. He would wake up at dawn, go for a morning stroll around the magnificent mountains, give the homeless food, listen to their struggles, and help as many of the destitute as possible. At home, he had a loving family, a beautiful wife, Sarah, and two sons: Ash and Scott. All of them were humble devotees of the Church of Scientology. Besides family and religion, he was a corporate consultant and worked to progress shares and spread business awareness.

His online life was a dream for family men from all walks of life. A balanced life was an achievement for middle-class workers because many struggled to provide a living for their family while still trying to remain sane. However, as always, the Internet is best at deceiving others. What seems perfect online isn't always the reality. The same was true in Roland's case. The Pyramid had changed him.

The perfect routine had become too much to handle.

So, he changed his foundation, loosened the perfect threads, and came under the influence of free will individuals. His followers soon all left, and he became just another social media user.

As time went on, he started spending more and more time on the Pyramid. Whenever he had spare time, he hopped onto the live videos of others or chatted with online friends. This created a barrier between him and his family. His wife felt neglected; his sons stopped sharing stories about themselves. Everything just went cold.

To gain positive support from his haters, he started disassociating from the Church of Scientology by claiming that it was overly restrictive and conservative. He became a Pyramid controversy, with posts solely for constant appreciation and approval from others. With this continuous desire for Internet credibility, his marriage failed, and he lost custody of his two sons. Instead of moving away from his addiction, he became more and more fixated on finding solace in the dark pit filled with empty faces.

This rapidly escalated in the media, but the Pyramid controlled the news from breaking the peace of its users, and the analytics team was asked to take care of the matter as swiftly as possible.

"Don't you think we should do something about this rapid shift?" Dan asked Matthew Tucker, one of his colleagues.

"I don't know, man," Matthew answered. "They have every single piece of information on us. I don't think we can do anything about this." There was a devastating sound of premonition in his voice. "I think you should stop prying and stay low. Otherwise, you might lose your job, Dan."

"Ugh, if I could only do something about this. I don't want to bear the guilt of ruining so many lives." Dan clasped his hands behind his neck, rubbing a sore spot there.

"I know, Dan, I know." Matthew patted his friend on the back as he stood up from his chair to get another cup of coffee.

That's when Michael barged into the room, holding out the report regarding Roland Brook.

"Why are we covering their tracks? This is outrageous!" Michael screamed as he threw the papers onto the table. "This is the second report I have to cover up this week. If this continues, we'll be considered a cult."

"That's exactly what I've been saying for a while now, but I guess we just have to do as we're told," Dan said mockingly while looking at Soha, who entered right after Michael.

"Don't look at me, Dan," she said scornfully. "I don't have any control over this situation, and let's face it, what do you think you can do about this, anyway? Kairi is too powerful." She shrugged her shoulders and leaned against one of the bookshelves in the room. "And the pay is good."

"Everyone, listen," Tara called for attention as she stood from her desk and walked over to the printer. The media manager had sent her some files to analyze, and her blood chilled at the news.

"Well, there's gotta be something we can do," Dan continued.

"Excuse me? I need your attention!" Tara yelled as her tall physique approached them with printed papers.

"What is it?" Michael asked as he grabbed one of them.

"I hate to break this to you, but we have another case." Tara sighed. "Nyla Richman. Her house burned down recently, and there is some negativity circling this case," Tara spoke as she held out the report to the rest of them.

Michael looked over at Dan and felt like screaming, but kept it inside.

"Yeah, I know about her," said Freya as she entered the room with a box full of doughnuts. "She gained her fame after debuting in Henry Gills' trilogy, and a few months ago, she openly posted her support and opinions on marginalized topics. She even fought for LGBTQ communities and other minority groups."

She looks so beautiful in that yellow dress, Dan thought, a little distracted from the issue at hand.

"She even had a law degree," Freya continued.

"A very influential woman," Soha added with her gray eyes wide open. "What happened to her, Tara?"

"Well, just like the other victims, she got heavily involved in the Pyramid," Tara began. "However, she lost her way as she gained popularity. Her acting skills weakened, which lost her a role in a colossal film. Her influence dropped. The change became evident. This concerned her friends and family. She was using the Pyramid excessively, hooked on reviewing and reading harsh comments on her change. All of a sudden, her cohesive arguments became vague, and nothing made sense anymore. Her opinions also became extreme. She stopped talking with her colleagues, she was no longer supporting the minorities, just arguing with the people who went against her."

"In short," Dan broke in, "she stopped caring about the needs of others?"

"Yeah." Tara looked over at Dan and nodded slightly.

Then she dropped the report on the table as a wave of guilt cascaded over her like a violent storm.

"I'm telling you. We need to stop this, or else we'll be trapped," Dan begged with a grave concern on his face as he looked over at the others.

Freya looked at him with a slight grin on her face, and he wondered what that was about.

From the other side, Soha looked at Freya closely with

a suspicious look on her face. The grin was quickly washed away and replaced with concern and anger.

Freya stared off into the distance, chewing on the inside of her cheek. All of this was playing around in her head. Rattling her mind, gnawing at her core. The stories of Richman and Brook had left a sinking feeling in her stomach. It reminded her too much of her own family history. She had come from a close-knit family where everyone got along.

Then something shifted. Social media came into their lives, and slowly, the unit began splitting at the seams, and soon, Freya found herself sitting at the dinner table all alone. No presents waiting for her under the tree at Christmas. Instead, she found her parents in bed, staring at their screens, obsessed with whatever their dead eyes had to offer them by way of imagined happiness.

She had also stopped hearing from her extended adopted family members. The Moores had plenty of aunts and uncles, cousins and nephews, and most of them seemed to have vanished. She watched them continue to post online, but never any direct communication.

The same happened to her few friends. Freya never had many friends, but she had lots of acquaintances, both in high school and college, but they had all vanished as well. For every posed picture on the Pyramid, another so-called friend dropped off the radar.

Eventually, Freya had found herself all alone. Her parents divorced, and there was no one left to turn to. It created a hunger inside of her, stirring the bad memories from her first few years in foster care. A hunger for vengeance on the entity that had brought destruction to her social life. The very object that was supposed to bring people together had torn her world apart.

CHAPTER FOUR

The tide of the world was changing. It was as if the sky, which in the past harbored rainbows, had been replaced by permanent grayness and an eerie silence that indicated a storm had wiped away the last glimmer of humanity's sanity. The joyous and welcoming society had turned gray — the colors faded away in hopes of rebirth, but in truth, there was no hope. This world had become a toxic dump.

Failure and success were both victims of criticism; it

didn't matter who lost or who won. Now, success depended on the approval of the soulless Pyramid.

"Freya, what are you reading?" her brother, Cyrus, asked as he sat next to her on a white L-shaped sofa. He was a tall, muscular man with wild brown hair and a sharp jawline, every bit of him a Philip Marlowe.

"It's the latest article written by Fatema Noor, a critical author of The Times," Freya explained. "It's on the social parasites." Her eyes were glued to her tablet while she spoke to him.

"Man, you read some weird things," Cyrus huffed, pulling out his phone and scrolling through the Pyramid app.

"It's reality," Freya replied as she put on her headphones and threw a sideways glance at him. She really despised her family's obsession with social media.

The article spoke about the need of people to please with looks. How young boys started going to the gym earlier and earlier, trying to obtain the perfect bodies they see on models on the app. It also explained how women usually had it worse, and how diet culture was ruining society. The beauty market had exploded, sales being higher than ever, and all types of diet pills, diet regimens, and beauty products were skyrocketing in sales.

This was all made worse by the fact that most models on the Pyramid had concessions from all the biggest brands, showing all the products and encouraging people to buy them in order to look just like them. Being able to buy products straight from the app with a simple click was paramount to this industry's rise.

Individuality was lost to a society that had turned into a mass of clones, all trying to look the same. All trying to pursue the same goals.

Freya had the habit of jotting down whatever she read online that was related to the negatives of social media, and surprisingly, she came across a lot of it. After all, the sole purpose of her joining the Pyramid corporation was to know how they influenced everyone so blindly, so the more information she could gather, the better.

"Did you know that many countries are concerned by the shifting patterns social media is creating?" Freya asked Cyrus, who was more interested in the viral video he was watching. "North Korea took an aggressive measure to restrict the Pyramid based on their bitter ties with America. The Chinese government considers westernization a parasite. And here you are, being sucked into it like a mindless being."

"Stop diving so much into this, Freya." Cyrus sighed as he lazily continued to scroll. "It's just an app."

"Ignore the issues all you want," Freya retorted. "But if something bad happens, don't come running to me."

She rose from her seat and stormed out of the room.

Cyrus ignored his sister's latest rant and focused on the bright glow of his screen. He lazily scrolled up and down, not quite certain what he was looking at or searching for. Images of people at the gym, flexing their muscles, flashed by, as did pictures of various meals or people in impossible yoga positions. He felt a gnawing sensation in the back of his mind, almost as if there were something he should be concerned about, or someone, but he ignored it as he kept scrolling.

A moment later, he paused, his sister's face dancing in his mind. Had she just been there? Was she upset about something? The more he tried to think about it, the more it faded from his mind, and his eyes wandered from staring at the wall to landing back at his phone and the warm shelter of social media.

Within a few minutes, he had completely forgotten about Freya again.

———

"KAIRI!" NICK HARRIDAN, A LARGE AND TOUGH MAN IN his mid-thirties, yelled as he made his way into her office. "Kairi, where are you?"

He turned to her assistant, and she informed him that he could wait in her office as Kairi had yet to return from a meeting.

The office was decorated with little furniture. The white and beige wallpaper matched the crimson and gray furniture and made the area spacious. There was a round coffee table in the center, while Kairi's chair sat in the right-hand corner of the room with her framed certificates hanging in neat rows behind the desk on the wall. Nick waited on the couch while Kairi took her sweet time coming back.

"What's up, Nick?" Kairi asked when she finally returned.

"Well, for one, congratulations on your promotion," he said in a sarcastic tone. "You took my spot. Dad would be proud of you. Second, there was a lot of commotion and a slight disagreement within the company, so I investigated, and guess what? The Pyramid is ruining people's lives!" he said in a sarcastic tone. "I wonder who the mastermind behind it could be?" He looked at her while sipping his tea from the paper cup he had brought from the cafeteria.

Kairi wanted to throw him out the window. Nick was her twin brother, and somehow, always came second. He was never able to win at anything. This jealous rivalry quickly turned into animosity. Even after their father's death, Cabal had been handed over to Kairi for her exceptionally powerful and intellectual capabilities — and maybe some influence from her side. Unlike her father, who had run most of that business from the island and away from the family, Kairi had decided to stay right in the middle of it. To be the one also running the Pyramid and getting her hands dirty, so to speak.

She'd given a spot to her brother not because they were close, or because she cared, but rather out of sheer curiosity of what he could do. And he had done well enough. Even if his intellect was beneath Kairi's, it was still above the average working mind.

"I have no idea what you're talking about." Kairi pointed him to the door. "And if you don't have any other gibberish to say, then you might as well leave."

"Oh, no, Kairi, I just came here to say hello." He continued to sip his tea, no intention of moving. "No need to feel threatened or bothered. I just came for some answers." He gave her a slight smirk, and then added, "If you don't want to answer, then don't bother. I don't want to trouble the famous Kairi. Smart move, right sis?"

He grinned and rose from the seat.

Kairi clenched her teeth in anger but forced a smile.

"Well, then excuse yourself," she said.

———

LATER THAT DAY, NICK MET UP WITH THE DIRECTOR TO arrange a meeting so all the recent casualties could be discussed, so that they could further cover up his sister's tracks.

The department heads gathered in their usual concealed meeting room without the presence of any outsiders. Armed guards locked the door, and Nick proceeded.

"Listen, everyone," he said in an oratory fashion. "I know this is a rushed meeting, but the current database has shown immense negativity due to the Pyramid. Even though we are trying our best to conceal the errors, there are still downfalls that I'm sure can be covered up by our experienced team." He gestured to the head of the public relations department. "I want reports from each department on what we can do to resolve this," he continued. "Otherwise, the company might experience some cuts."

"Sir," the head of internal affairs began. "There is a slight revolt within the company. People can see through the control that's being held upon them."

"Fire everyone who shows any sign of revolt, or make them sign an NDA." Nick slammed his fist onto the glass table. "If they still show any sign of disagreement, then instantly eliminate them. We don't want anyone revolting against Cabal." Nick stared at the assembled heads with fiery eyes.

"Yes, sir," everyone replied unanimously.

As the meeting concluded, everyone departed.

"Taking the elevator?" a familiar voice asked behind Nick.

He turned around and saw Atlas Zayn, the head delegate, and the man he knew Kairi had been infatuated with for a very long time. Naturally, Nick knew everything when it came to his sister's endeavors.

"Sure." Nick smiled, and they walked over together.

The building had fourteen floors, each dedicated to a separate department. As the elevator reached the thirteenth floor, Nick ushered the handsome man inside. There was an uncomfortable silence between them until Nick finally broke it.

"So, did you enjoy today's meeting?"

"Yeah, it was interesting," Atlas replied curtly. "A bit too urgent, perhaps. But I know Kairi wants to make sure everything is in order before we launch the new update,"

"A new launch?" Nick asked casually, trying not to sound surprised.

"The prototype is not ready yet," Atlas kept going, "but definitely, in three months, there will be something thrilling out in the world."

"Hmm, that's interesting," Nick replied. "The launch will be the most exciting event this year, I suppose."

"Definitely," Atlas replied as the elevator stopped on the ground floor.

They looked at each other for a moment, then nodded by way of goodbye before parting ways.

A new launch, Nick thought. *This is going to cast the world further into chaos.*

Unlike Kairi, he had a heart, and this news worried him.

The heaven that the Pyramid had always promised was not real. It was far from the safest place on Earth. It was, in reality, one of the worst places out there. The app would go on supporting its users and encouraging them to make sure that they felt satisfied with their own reality, but in the end, the designers behind it corrupted the poor pure souls who believed the lie.

But why didn't the people stop it? If all the incidents reported on the news clearly showed this, why did it keep going? Why didn't anybody see this coming? The short answer to this would be that their behavior was reinforced by the app. Instead of addressing the decline of these once important influencers, the public promoted their failed lifestyles. Looking at them as if they had casted off the shackles of an oppressive world.

This was the problem with posting a life online and indulging heavily in it. Right and wrong only became a matter of opinion, likes, comments, and shares. On the other hand, it introduced a bandwagon effect on the digital level. The Pyramid feed was highlighted by everything and anything; it could be right, wrong, true, or false. Yet, all that was irrelevant to the approval of the people. Perceptions became corrupt, ideas became stagnant, and critical thinking degraded as people injured themselves for clout to the level that supported their failed existence.

IT WAS LATE WHEN CLARISSA SAT ON THE FLOOR OF Kairi's office again and took a selfie from high above. The musty, ancient scrolls and books spread out on the office floor could be seen behind her. She took a few extra from other angles, just to be on the safe side. She checked the screen and smiled, then proceeded to post it on the Pyramid with #historybuff. She was well aware of what the app was doing to common folks out there, but the urge to show the world what she was up to was too strong to ignore. Her family had laughed at her when she announced what she wanted to do for a living, and this was her way of showing them that it wasn't a waste of time. That she was a success, that she was working for one of the biggest companies out there.

She remained on the floor after posting the picture and scrolled through the hashtag she had just posted. Looking at other history students, professors, or plain lovers. There were lots of images of architecture, artifacts, or ancient places. She felt a twinge of jealousy. She also wanted to be at all those places. The places she had read about in college.

As the office lights dimmed hours later, she was still sitting there, staring at the accomplishments of others.

CHAPTER FIVE

Cyrus woke up with a splitting headache early the next morning. He rolled out of bed, reached for his phone, and opened the Pyramid app while sitting on the edge of the mattress. He tried to roll his head from side to side in order to loosen his neck, but he couldn't shake the pain. After scrolling through the feed, he opened the camera and took a selfie to post on his story.

He was taken aback when he saw the pale image looking back at him.

"What the hell?" He erased the image.

He took another, and then looked at it as well. His face looked rough, pudgy, and shapeless, milky white skin dropping in a jowly fashion around his mouth. His eyes were cloudy and white, as if he were wearing contacts.

He posted the image anyway with #feelinglikeshit, and then headed to the bathroom in order to do his morning routine. His legs felt unsteady as he moved, as if they were stiffer than usual. He really hoped he wasn't coming down with something.

———

"Look what I just found." Keenan picked up a file hidden at the back of a rusty, old filing cabinet. It was still early morning, and they'd been in that dusty room for almost an hour.

"What is it?" Clarissa turned around and stepped off the ladder. She had been submerged in the cabinets on the opposite wall for a while. Everything around her smelled papery and musty, and she struggled not to sneeze.

"I don't know, but it's got this logo on it." Keenan held up the file to show it to her. "Isn't it similar to Cabal's?"

Clarissa grabbed the old folder, dusted it off, and then opened it. She flipped through the pages to find that everything was written in some ancient language she couldn't understand. It almost looked like some kind of cipher.

"We should visit the historical association and get them to analyze this." Clarissa held the file close to her chest, as if her whole life depended on the ancient treasure. "Did you find anything else?"

"Yeah, I just came across the treasure you're holding." He smiled as if he had just told the world's best joke.

"Keenan, that's not funny. We don't have time for jokes right now."

"Clarissa, what if we find something that shouldn't be found?" Keenan looked at her with his intense eyes, suddenly serious, almost as if he knew something Clarissa didn't. "Kairi gives such weird vibes sometimes. I don't know if I trust her with restricted and dangerous information."

Clarissa paused momentarily. The indulgent thought of going against the orders of Kairi Harridan scared her, but she knew Keenan had a point. Kairi would most likely abuse the information.

"I don't know, Keenan, I don't know." She sighed and rubbed her eyes, feeling exhausted and drained.

"Are you feeling alright?" Keenan touched her arm, and she jumped a little.

"What do you mean?"

"You look a bit pale, and there are dark circles under your eyes."

"Just a late night yesterday, long day today." Clarissa picked up her phone and turned on the camera in order to look at herself.

She couldn't even remember how long she had been on the Pyramid the previous day. Her eyes were sunken in, and her skin pale and milky white. She snapped a picture to post later. #latenight

———

In 2070, Kairi became the CEO of Cabal. The entity had many robust employees, but Kairi's ruthlessness and strict principles had taken her to the top.

She was also the one to have perfectly engineered the

Pyramid's algorithm in order to make it the central hub of society. An entity that judged, formulated, and compared trends while also allowing Cabal to attain its objective of world domination.

But now, Kairi could tell that there was something going on behind her back. She didn't like the revolt within her company, and she saw the cracks showing up in her kingdom.

Her intercom beeped, and Kelly, her secretary, announced that she was coming in with some urgent information.

Kairi leaned forward on her desk, and the door opened up almost straight away. Kelly wasn't just Kairi's secretary; she was also her right hand when it came to finding solutions. She was the mirror image of Kairi, which meant that she was extraordinarily manipulative and cunning, and had an endearing appearance that could get anyone under her thumb.

"Kairi, the cases are rapidly increasing," the secretary said as she sat down on the other side of the desk and placed a pile of papers on top of it. "We need to do something about this before our next launch if we want to make sure everyone gets the new update."

"I was thinking about having a more direct approach," Kairi replied as she rifled through the most recent cases that Kelly had placed before her. "It might be slightly costly, but we can cover the loss. We need to reach out to these aspiring influencers and give them a public forum so that we can make them our pawns. We have to make sure that they reach out globally through their posts and discuss how the Pyramid changed their lives, how it made them into somebody, from nobody. We need a few cases like this to raise back the awareness of the positive impact the Pyramid is having on society."

"A dream come true for them." Kelly smirked.

"Precisely," Kairi agreed. "If people are able to see that the Pyramid is changing lives and benefiting people, we will overpower the critics."

Kelly nodded before leaving the office and running to grab a list of their potential targets.

———

FREYA FOUND THE OFFICE MUCH QUIETER THAN NORMAL that night when she came in for her night shift. She didn't do those often, but as an intern, she sometimes had to cover when people didn't show up. Freya always put her hand up for these shifts, as it gave her an opportunity to spend more time in the office at a time when less people were around. This time, the memo had come at the last minute, when she was already at home, but she returned to the office regardless. At night, she had better chances of finding things out. After all, she was still a woman with a mission.

She tried searching for someone from the social media team to tell her what she was supposed to do that night, but found it difficult to track anyone down. It wasn't until she reached the cafeteria that she found them.

A group of employees were sitting around an oval table, staring at their phones. They had all decided to eat dinner together, for plastic containers with various dishes were laid out before them, but it was all untouched. Whatever they were looking at on their phones seemed far more engaging than their food.

"Excuse me," Freya said in a soft, yet audible, voice.

Nothing happened. The figures didn't move at all, except for thumbs scrolling along the screens.

"Hello," she said again, this time louder.

As she spoke, she saw a flicker in the eye of another intern, Paul. Like a twitch in the corner of his eye, almost as if he wanted to acknowledge her but couldn't. Then his mouth fell open, and he let out a low gargle, not quite a moan, not quite a word — just a rattle of saliva in the back of his throat.

At this, the other employees around the table suddenly moved. Their eyes flicked from side to side in an erratic movement. Freya walked over to inspect them, and as she moved around the table, they seemed to follow her with more than just their eyes. But their hands were still clutched to their phones. Freya made sure not to touch them, as she wasn't sure what was going on.

She went in for a closer look at Paul, who appeared to have it worse than the rest of them. His skin had turned paper white, and with the sheen of sweat covering it, he almost looked transparent. His once bright blue eyes were dull and almost pale, and his pupils had taken on a gray quality. He followed her finger as she held it up to him, unfocused. His breath reeked of rot, like a bag of garbage left out in the sun for a week.

"I don't think you're well," Freya muttered as she backed away from the intern and wrinkled her nose. "I would see a doctor if I were you. In fact, I think you should all go see your doctors." She was almost in a daze, knowing that something was very wrong but unable to process it.

She pointed to the others around the table before she slowly moved away from the cafeteria. So, it was finally happening. Their obsession with the Pyramid had fully gotten to them. She always knew this day would come. Things had been escalating for months, and it was all finally collapsing. She had seen something like this happen with her family, how the social media platform had sucked them in and turned them mindless, but this was on another level.

As she turned away, she paused for a moment. Something tugged at her. Maybe she needed to do something to help them. Take their phones and toss them out the window to break the spell. If she severed the bond between man and app, would they start taking care of themselves and go to the doctor? Take a day off to recuperate? She couldn't know.

In the end, she concluded that they'd all brought this upon themselves, and they deserved it. Freya shrugged her shoulders and continued to walk away. As she moved through the building, she came upon other employees in similar states. Sitting motionless at their desks, engulfed by the Pyramid. Not everyone seemed to have caught it, but enough for her to imagine that one employee had gotten sick, and without care, brought it into work.

With their minds on the Pyramid, the infected had forgotten to care.

Fuck them, Freya thought. *They'll have to fend for themselves.*

———

KAIRI STOOD BY THE WINDOW OF HER CONDO. HER mansion was on the other side of Santa Cruz, but as it was an hour drive from Menlo Park — home of the Pyramid headquarters — she often stayed in her condo instead. Or, if she felt pressed for time and needed to be at the mansion, she used her helicopter to get there.

The window looked over the ocean, and it was her usual place of comfort, her safe zone. The kind of place she tried to convince the public that the Pyramid could be for them. Tonight, she stood there, bouncing on her heels with a cup of tea in her hands, taking in the beauty of the natural world. She felt grounded, centered every time she looked out over the great expanse. The vastness of dark and untamed nothingness, the opposite of the cold harsh world she wanted to create for others. The sea could barely be distinguished from the sky, the stars reflecting on it and making it almost look like she was drifting in space.

Her tranquility was interrupted when she heard the footsteps of her brother coming from behind her.

"Hey, sis." He placed a hand on the small of her back. "Sorry to bother you, but they let me in, and I need to ask you something."

Kairi sipped her tea in short, measured mouthfuls and continued to stare out the window, but instead of watching the ocean move back and forth in wild waves, she saw his reflection instead.

"What is it?" she replied curtly after the long pause. "It's almost midnight, not a normal time to come over for a chat, is it?"

"Well, I won't beat around the bush as I have a meeting early in the morning, and I need to head home. I just finished a long double shift to try and get some extra work done." He moved to stand next to her, also staring out toward the ocean. "So, tell me, what is this new launch that has everyone talking?"

That was the thing with her brother. Like her, he

always went straight to the point. She hated that trait in other people, but in her, it was a great way to get answers.

Almost no one knows about the launch, just close members of the team. What's he talking about? Kairi thought.

"The launch?" she replied in a calm voice, trying to make it sound like a surprise. "Well, we are just updating some features, that's all. I would hardly call it a new launch."

"Kairi, I know you and how mischievous you can get with plans, and I know your goal is world domination. I'm not stupid." He waved his hands in the air as if this were something they talked about on the daily. "Of course, even Cabal is part of this plan, but you're going to go overboard with everything as you often do, aren't you?"

He turned to look at her. Kairi tightened her jaw as she felt his eyes boring into her.

"No, it's under control, brother," she said, still trying to keep calm. "Don't worry. It's just an update."

An update that will get us all the power, my brother. All the power we have always wanted and deserved, she thought as she continued to watch the magic of unfiltered nature unfold before her.

———

CLARISSA LOOKED AT HER LATEST IMAGE ON HER Pyramid feed as she lied in bed that night. It was almost midnight, and she knew she was supposed to be asleep already, but she couldn't stop looking at her feed. There was something off about that picture. She had always prided herself on being very put together. Unlike the other history nerds, she wasn't mousy with glasses and dull, lifeless hair. No, she was tan, with dark hair and a vivacious look, every bit the envy of any librarian in the world.

She could *wow* men with her intellect, as well as her body. Yet, the image she had just taken showed a different person — haggard and pasty. She had deep dark circles around her eyes, looking almost dead. She turned the camera to selfie mode again and inspected her appearance, touched her sad-looking skin, slapping it to get some color back into her cheeks.

Then she found it.

A small patch of dry, flaking skin on her chin, just below the mouth. She scratched at it, pulled a little, but the patch just became bigger and bigger, and soon, she was able to pull off a big chunk of skin, exposing the raw meat underneath.

"What the...?"

The action hadn't hurt at all. She had simply torn a piece of herself off, and it hadn't hurt.

———

SOMETHING WAS GOING ON; CYRUS COULD FEEL IT. HE looked over at the clock radio on his nightstand. It was midnight. Suddenly, his Pyramid feed had turned screwy. The people he followed began to post strange images. Like the flick of a switch, the selfies had all turned from gorgeous images of healthy and beautiful people doing inspirational things to the same people staring vacantly at themselves in a bathroom mirror.

Cyrus scrolled through the timeline of one of the women he usually followed — her pictures were almost like a strange animation, her skin transforming from a pale white to a sickly green. Her eyes turning from clear blue to cloudy and white. Her teeth going from pearly white to stained yellow.

Cyrus pushed on her most recent story, and up popped a video showing her peeling the skin off her arm. The flesh looked decayed and rancid, easily coming off and exposing muscle and bone beneath. It looked gross, but she didn't seem to react to the action she was performing, and it made Cyrus nauseous.

He moved to another person, to another feed, only to see the same thing. Greenish appearance, rotten teeth, and torn skin. All of a sudden, his notifications blew up. The Pyramid was flooded with images of people turning.

CHAPTER SIX

10 hours earlier

"**D**on't tell me you found the restricted documents." Keenan looked surprised as Clarissa called him in for an emergency meeting. "Clarissa, these all have the logo of Cabal from 1880."

"I know, Keenan, and I made a copy and sent these to Kairi already." Clarissa steadied herself against her desk as she found it increasingly difficult to keep her balance. "I know you warned me, but I'm simply her employee. What else am I supposed to do?"

Clarissa tried to justify her behavior, but they both knew it was a risky road they were heading down. But Clarissa had been too scared of the repercussions if Kairi were to find out that she was hiding information from her.

"I don't know what to say," Keenan replied. "Let's just pray nothing bad happens. Does anyone else know about this?"

"No, no one; it's highly confidential." Clarissa wiped her forehead with a handkerchief.

Keenan came over and gave her a hug; her body felt warm and sweaty through her clothes, and there was an unmistakable smell of garbage and putrefaction about her. It made him wrinkle his nose, but he didn't let go. She probably just stepped on something foul.

"It's fine," he said and patted her on the back. "Don't feel guilty. I hope there isn't anything dangerous related to the artifact."

Clarissa thought his hug felt like home. Warm and familiar, like a summer day, and she welcomed it. She felt discombobulated and was having a difficult time keeping her mind on one thought.

"Keenan, the artifact... It will change the world. People will lose their minds." She started sobbing, unable to keep her fear inside any longer.

"Hey, hey, what do you mean by that?" Keenan tried to comfort her as best he could, not quite sure what she was getting at.

"It is linked to the War of Rusziye," she replied through her tears, unable to explain the full extent of what she feared.

There was only silence afterwards. Keenan didn't say

anything. He backed away from her, and then just stood there, looking at her blankly.

———

THE DOCUMENTS WERE DELIVERED TO THE DEPARTMENT within minutes. The courier took them to the front desk and specifically stated the urgency of the papers reaching their destination. The administrator took them to the office, where Kairi sat in a state of shock after the discovery.

Slowly, she came up with the perfect plan to release the virus into the world, so that everything would fall under her control.

She buzzed Kelly into the room.

"Kelly, the documents from the archives have arrived, and it is exactly what we predicted." Excitement radiated from Kairi like the warm glow of the newly discovered artifact.

"With this, we can conquer the world, right?" Kelly was astonished as Kairi pulled out the artifact from her locked drawer.

"Yes, but we need to alter it first. We want control, not an apocalypse," Kairi stated.

"Okay," Kelly replied. "I will alert the team to join, and you can work on the objectives."

"Wait." Kairi halted her before she headed out of the room. "I was thinking... What if we make it into a molecular weapon, something that penetrates the skin? Maybe we can release the virus via the screen, and that way, we can get enough radiation to manipulate people's thought process?"

"Seems a bit risky..." Kelly paused on the threshold.

"Though we can make a prototype and test it before the actual launch?" she suggested. "Maybe we could even test it here with a few close members or interns that we can monitor in person?"

"Okay." Kairi bit her cheek for a moment. "Gather the team, and we'll have a discussion about it."

She didn't want to admit that Kelly was right. It *was* a risk, but if things went south, she could just blame it on her.

———

AT THE OFFICE, EVERYONE WAS HUSTLING. WHEN NICK arrived, his presence wasn't demeaning or strict like Kairi's usually was. Instead, everyone welcomed him with a happy smile on their face. Things were calmer when he was around, less chaotic.

Freya watched him as he came out of the elevator. She felt inevitably attracted to him — he was the most beautiful man she had ever seen. His muscles flexed under his rolled-up sleeves; he had broad shoulders, and the subtle definition of a six pack could barely be seen hiding below the white shirt.

Nick crossed the room toward his desk when his eyes met Freya's; he gave her a warm smile and went into his office.

"Why doesn't he come here more often?" Soha asked as she pined over him in admiration.

"Yeah," whispered Freya.

"Oh, honey, you're blushing," Soha teased. "Do you have a crush on Nick Harridan?" Soha didn't wait for a reply and returned to her seat.

"No, I don't," Freya called back to her.

"You don't what?" asked a husky, deep voice from behind them.

Freya turned, and her heart dropped; Nick was standing right behind her!

"Nothing, sir," Freya stammered. "We were just having a discussion."

She cowered away from his big, hulking frame, and with it, awkwardness consumed her.

"Okay..." He paused for a moment as if searching his memory for a name while raising a perfectly sculpted eyebrow.

"Freya, her name is Freya Moore," Soha interjected and broke some of the tension.

He nodded at Soha, an unreadable look on his face as he then bit his lip, opened and closed his mouth, and finally said, "You're not a permanent employee here, are you?"

"No, just an intern at the moment," Freya responded and turned her head. "I've only been here for a couple of weeks."

"Freya..." Nick smiled once she turned back to look at him, and he gave her a quick once-over. Something about that name sounded strangely familiar, but he couldn't put a pin on it. "Anyway, Freya Moore, I'm in need of a new assistant. I know a lot of interns are looking to stay here permanently, so would you like to be my secretary?"

Freya's jaw dropped, and her heart sank into the pit of her stomach.

Is this how he flirts? she thought.

"Wow, I-I'm grateful," she said, trying to hide her ecstatic joy. "Thank you so much, sir."

"No worries, see you in my office on Monday?" He phrased the last part as a question.

"Yes, sir," Freya replied with an elevated voice.

Nick grinned at her before closing the glass door to the room, and she watched him stroll back to his own desk.

The others joined them soon after, all revolving around Freya like curious flies drawn to the light.

"What was that about, Freya Moore?" Michael teased, saying her full name in a mocking tone, as if copying Nick.

Dan looked a bit lost and weirded out. "He's a flirt, so just be careful," he said with a jealous tone.

"I know, guys." Freya grinned. "Thanks, Dan, I will keep that in mind... But, guys, did I just get a job as Nick Harridan's secretary? I'm a permanent employee now!"

Her face now exuded pure excitement and confidence. She was proud of herself but didn't really know why.

"Hey, do we have information on the launch we're planning?" Dan asked, wanting to change the topic.

"No, but we got a memo saying Kairi will hold a meeting with the board of directors today to discuss the new interventions in the algorithm," Michael informed the room. "He was complaining that Kairi keeps on reformatting the structure again and again."

"I wonder what else they are cooking up in that mansion," Freya spat out as she angrily looked over at Nick's office, unable to keep in her venom.

Soha stopped to think for a moment. To her, Freya was an enigma that she just couldn't wrap her head around. Just moments ago, she was drooling over Nick, and now, she was resenting the entire crew, even the charismatic Mr. Harridan. In time, she would crack her; she was sure of it.

———

Kairi worked on a memo to be sent only to the most high-ranking executive members of Cabal before their meeting. The group consisted of experts from every field, and the memo was about directing their resources into researching the possibility of developing and weaponizing devices that could influence minds to make them more inclined toward the Pyramid. She had an undetectable device, which would attack the nervous system or spinal nerves without causing any physical damage to the humans, which she planned on adding to their devices.

"Ms. Kairi, everyone is ready for you in the conference hall," Kelly informed her, poking her head through the office door.

"I'm coming," Kairi replied as she picked up her things and went into the meeting room.

As Kairi entered, the space fell silent. She was dressed in her usual attire of straight lines with no frills, a true power outfit, and it only added to her already powerful presence. The room had directors and heads in charge of the tech, design, and security departments, and they all looked at her as she strode in.

She talked them through the entire process and guided them through the algorithm they were supposed to work on.

The following list emerged on the white screen:

Emit a strong radiofrequency-electromagnetic field that targets the nervous system.

The addictive algorithm that controls the human subconscious.

No physical harm.

Interlink people's lives with this application.

The patterns should change after the user reaches 10k followers.

"This is going to be the prototype of our next update," Kairi said proudly. "We will run the algorithm on a few individuals before taking things to a grander scale," she concluded as she clicked away the presentation.

"What do you mean by controlling the human subconscious?" the man in charge of security asked with a light frown.

"It's just a metaphor, Mr. Thompson." Kairi tried to flash a darling smile. "We want to make sure that people get addicted to the system. That way, we will be able to amplify our sales and gain full control."

"So, you want us to create an interface that releases a radiofrequency?" the director of the tech department scratched his chin.

"Yes, sir." Kairi turned to the wispy little man dressed in an oversized suit. "According to our recent developments, it is possible to release waves via the interface," she explained.

"I am aware of this, Ms. Kairi, but what about the harm it could cause?" the director continued.

"That is why it is a pilot trial." The smile was becoming increasingly difficult to maintain. "We will only test on a few individuals before anything becomes official."

The man nodded and clasped his hands in front of himself on the desk.

He is still tense, Kairi thought. These damn caring humans. *I will have to monitor him and his behavior.*

"We are going to make sure everything stays inside this room; not even an ounce of this discussion leaves here," Kelly stated. "You are all obliged to sign this non-disclosure agreement." She passed everyone a printed document. "You should all read it before signing, if you please."

When Kairi left the meeting room, she spoke with

Kelly and told her to release the prototype to the small team she had selected for testing. Kelly wasn't too happy when Kairi told her to stay and work a double shift in order to monitor the workers herself, but she did it for the greater good. She did it because she believed in everything that Kairi had told her.

CHAPTER SEVEN

After the meeting adjourned, a memo was sent to all the executive board members. The team worked extensively day and night to get the algorithm changed and running without any issues. The first prototype was sent to Kairi in the early hours of the night, and then the night team kept working on improving it.

The next morning, a few team members left, but a few others came in. Between them all, they kept working on the last adjustments, making sure they could have everything done as fast as possible as Kairi had asked.

But nearing the end of the process, something unimaginable happened.

It was early afternoon when the graphic designer began developing the new logo for the Pyramid based on an old artifact that Cabal had possessed in the 15th Century. Cabal had many such artifacts in its possession; they were all remnants of their past struggles, triumphs, and even failures.

This particular artifact was round, with a striped pattern embossed around the border. It was placed in a 3D printer for scanning and replicating. The designer began the scan, the machine made a sound, and he went toward it with a puzzled look on his face.

The artifact glowed inside the scanner, with beams emanating out of the engraved grooves. The computer screen went blurry, the window of the memo maximized on its own, and then the screen went blank.

On the other side of the building, data analysts and server administrators sat at their workstations and noticed the data flow and traffic of the Pyramid increase. This had never happened before... until now.

"Guys, what's happening?" Freya asked as she emerged from Nick's office after putting the latest reports on his desk. She was exhausted from pulling a double shift the day before, her mind feeling sluggish.

"We don't know; something has happened," Soha yelled. "A virus, maybe?"

"The super servers are unstable, and some have even crashed." Michael ran from screen to screen, frantically tapping the keyboard. "The traffic has increased too much, too rapidly."

"Hang on. I will contact the tech department and ask them."

He looked like a sweaty head with curly hair and round glasses as he headed for the nearest phone.

"They are saying an outbreak has occurred," Johnson Smith, one of the coders in the same room, said. "No one knows what happened."

I was afraid this might happen, Nick thought as he returned to his office. *Did they launch the new algorithm?*

He picked up the reports that Freya had placed on his desk, but simply threw them back without looking at them. He rubbed his tired eyes and slumped in his chair.

Freya came back into the office and looked at him with great concern, and he returned the sentiment.

———

A BLAST OF FIRE IGNITED IN THE IT DEPARTMENT, where they had started working on the algorithm for the new interface.

"Look at the smoke, Ryland," said one of the employees as he frantically moved away from his desk and stumbled onto the floor. "Look at all that smoke; we have to leave, now!" His voice escalated into a guttural crack as fear rose inside of him.

"Guys, the system is on fire," Erik said, looking up and seeing the smoke rise from the machinery.

Suddenly, the claxons started sounding — the alarm ringing in the entire department. The emergency exits automatically opened across their floor.

"Everyone, leave the room!" a voice called out. "Ryland, move away from the system. Kim Hyun, you too, get over here. There is nothing we can do about this. At any minute, there will be an explosion."

The sound reverberated throughout the whole floor

and pushed everything in various directions as an explosion took over the room. The systems failed, went offline. Smoke and fire spread everywhere, like a fiery dragon unfurling and stretching its long serpentine body in all directions while spewing red hot flames from its lethal maw.

When the emergency services reached the hub of it all, the entire team laid spread out across the floor, pushed far away from the system as it burned. The blast had taken a significant toll on the team, who were all confused at what had actually happened. Some were severely injured due to the intense electrical shocks, others were in shock and couldn't move their bodies because the rays produced were highly harmful, and they affected their minds — disconnecting their minds from their bodies.

Once the news reached Kairi, she quickly rushed to the scene and ordered the injured employees and bodies to be taken to Cabal's Medical Center rather than the regular hospitals nearby.

"I want everyone to keep quiet about this incident," she said to the gathered emergency personnel, hands on her hips with great presence. "We will label this as a fire outbreak and nothing more, okay?"

She wanted to keep the news about the incident hidden from the media in order to not spur up the opposition. A few notable engineers had lost their lives as they were the closest to the shockwaves. Other crew members were on their deathbeds and would most likely not survive.

Back at the Pyramid, the employees were in utter shock. No one knew how the ratings of the app had gone through the roof during the past eighteen hours.

"I'm telling you guys, something is very wrong with the system," said Dan as he panted heavily.

"Kairi must have done something," Soha replied as she unsteadily sipped her tea. "I wonder whether the tech team knew about the new update."

"No, Kim Hyun said they weren't informed about any update," Michael said, deleting his Pyramid account. "They *were* working on a new version of the app. But it wasn't ready to be tested. He suggested that we delete every Pyramid account for the time being."

"Do you think we should do something?" Dan asked. "I've sent out a report to the other teams to form a merger and end this system."

Dan sat with droopy shoulders and stared into his own cup of tea.

"It's going to be difficult," Soha replied with a shocked expression. "And you need to be careful; otherwise, who knows what Kairi might do. Don't you guys listen to the rumors?"

"No, what did she do now?" Michael asked.

"Don't say anything," Dan whispered and pointed to the glass window facing the corridor. "Someone's coming."

The door opened, and Freya walked in.

"Hey, did you guys hear about the fire?" she asked while pulling some files out from a black and white painted cabinet.

"Yeah, it's devastating," Soha replied. "They are saying an electrical shock burnt the entire IT department."

"I don't buy into the rumors," Freya said as she double checked the files. "There is something sinister going on. A new update went up on the Pyramid. No one knows who released it."

Dan kept his eyes on her the entire time. She fascinated him. There was something about her energy, and the way she walked. Even though she was just a secretary, she knew a surprising amount about the incident.

Soon, she exited the room, leaving the three of them staring at each other.

"The new launch," Soha said as soon as Freya disappeared. "She knew something about the launch."

"Yeah, she works for Nick Harridan now," Dan replied sarcastically.

"Are you getting jealous?" Michael asked upon hearing the tone in Dan's voice. "Do you like her?"

Yeah, I do, Dan thought in his mind. "Can you shut up?"

He rolled his eyes and smirked. "Yeah, you do."

"Anyway, how could they launch when nothing was ready?" Soha asked.

Suddenly, Dan's phone started ringing.

"I'm sure something happened." Dan looked at the caller ID and held up a finger. "I'm warning you guys; this is not good at all."

Dan walked off while Soha and Michael looked at one another with confusion.

THE PYRAMID USAGE CONTINUED TO GO OFF THE charts, and the criticism of it began to trend on the news outlets. Fox One had an anti-social media campaign, and this spike was a red flag for them. The conspiracy theorists spiraled out of control and lashed out with outrageous ideas and ideologies that further expedited the usage of the Pyramid.

Almost a full day after the catastrophe had taken place, the world fell into chaos. It felt like Chernobyl had reoccurred, but in the digital world instead. Extremely horrifying things began to happen. The people who barely used to use the Pyramid started to become addicted. They engaged in live sessions and would post every detail about their lives, from the minute they woke up to the minute they went back to sleep.

It was a wave of digital media usage that had never been witnessed before. Offices worldwide started experiencing a shortage of employees, and as a result, the stock market became disrupted, rendering the country's economy unstable in an instant.

Companies were forced to make other employees fill various critical positions to minimize the damage inflicted by the app. Many people refused to leave their homes, staying in bed instead to scroll through the Pyramid.

It confused Kairi, the Pyramid, and Cabal. What they had planned worked, the usage was soaring now, but they had never executed the design. No one had authorized the order, and no plan had been carried out for it. The interesting part of it all was that Kairi had no idea that this evolution occurred due to the artifact; they had a virus outbreak on their hands.

This development wasn't good, and because of it, an outcry rose in the ranks of the organization at the center of it all: Cabal.

The executives were terrified of getting exposed and decided to lay low. Instead, Kairi's personal phone began to blow up.

"You better pick up before they come knocking," Nick said as he crept around the corner.

"Why are you always in my house?" Kairi yelled at him. She was already distraught, and he just had to be there, prying.

"Oh, sis, calm down," he said and laughed. "I'm here to help."

"I don't need your help," Kairi huffed. "But I do need to fire the security guard who let you in."

"I can cover this up, Kairi. You don't have to be so stubborn all the time." He sat on the white loveseat with his hands clasped together in front of him. "You just need to tell me what you released."

"I don't know." Kairi looked away from him. "We weren't supposed to launch. It wasn't ready." Kairi fell silent for a few minutes. "Everything is under control," she finally continued. "I don't need your help. You're not even part of Cabal."

Kairi knew he would try anything to get under her skin, but she had to stay calm and not reveal a single thing. Otherwise, the entire plan would fall apart. *Did she even have a plan, still?* Things were getting out of control.

Kairi turned back to Nick angrily. "You *left* Cabal, and for the past five years since, I've been working every single day to keep things under control. Without you. So, don't worry. I don't *need* you."

"Kairi, I gotta be honest. I hate the methods you use at the organization." Nick leaned forward. "It only serves selfish purposes." He paused for a moment, gathering his thoughts and thinking of a better way to approach his sister. "I don't have any desire to rule the world," he continued. "So, there's no reason for you to worry, I won't take over. I'll fly under the radar so that I know when to cover up your mistakes for the sake of our father's memory."

Kairi stayed silent, looking out the window and thinking over Nick's words. After some time, she turned to him and spoke again.

"How's Mother?" Kairi asked. She had never gotten along with that woman, especially after their father's death.

"She's good." Nick sank back in his seat as he replied. "Better, in fact, and at peace. She asks about you all the time, you know?" Their mother had lost her mind some time ago, premature aging taking her mind along with a lot of her memories, but it was more often than not that she remembered Kairi and asked about her. "There is something she remembers once in a while, and she insists she wants to share it with you herself... you should go see her."

"Maybe in another life." Kairi turned back to the window, crossing her arms over her chest. "Anyway, I'll send you some files regarding an ancient artifact that we found. That's what we're working on. Until then, take care of the media."

Kairi turned back around and went to pour herself some wine.

"Wine? It's barely noon," Nick said in a mocking, but worried, voice.

"Leave," Kairi commanded, waving him away as if he were an annoying fly.

———

"Look at this," Soha said to Michael as she pointed to the jumbled mess of numbers scrolling up and down the screen.

"What am I looking at?" Michael asked.

"This is the code to the new update," Soha replied. She pointed to a cluster of numbers again. "This seems to be some form of subliminal code."

"Talk to me like I'm an idiot," Michael said, deadpanning at her.

"Somehow, the code can change the genetic makeup of a person." She looked at him. "It seems like the update can reprogram the brain of the individual who uses it. It shuts it down, causes it to eat itself somehow."

"What are you saying?" Michael looked puzzled.

"From what I can read in the code," Soha explained, scooting back with her chair, "this code will kill the brain, but still keep the body alive. It creates some kind of undead monster."

"You're joking!" Michael laughed, truly believing that Soha was playing a joke on him. "Is this a prank? Who's recording?" He looked about the room, but no one else was around.

"Not at all." Soha switched to a random Pyramid account to show Michael.

A woman had put up a story of herself ripping pieces of skin from her body, exposing the raw muscle beneath.

"Look at this!" She switched to another account, where a man had posted an image of himself looking in the mirror. His skin was pale, bordering on translucent, and his eyes yellow. "This is happening everywhere! The more they use the app, the more they start to decay. It has to be the new algorithm."

"Damn it," Michael called Dan over, who came running from the other room.

"What's going on?" Dan asked as he looked at the screen of the Pyramid accounts.

"We have a problem," Michael replied. "A huge problem. The new update is turning people into the walking dead."

"Stop it," Dan replied. "That's impossible."

"What do you call this, then?" Soha flipped through several accounts, each story or image worse than the one before it.

"We need to report this to Kairi." Michael turned to Dan. "We have to shut this down!"

"I'll give permission to do so." Dan looked at them both. "Even if it gets us all canned."

"Then we have to get to the main hub," Soha replied.

The trio headed down the winding corridors of the office building, down the stairs to the basement, only to stop at the great double doors that led to the machines housing the Pyramid's matrix.

"You know how to stop this?" Dan turned to Soha.

"I can do it in my sleep," she replied.

Dan unlocked the door with his key card, and the familiar buzz sounded to inform them that it was open.

"I wouldn't do that if I were you," Kairi said from behind them.

The three of them turned around to see her standing in the corridor, hands behind her back. She stood flanked by two guards carrying pistols.

"We need to shut down the system," Michael told her.

"What do you mean?" Kairi smiled at them deviously.

"The update is spreading some kind of virus," Soha pleaded. "It's turning people into monsters!"

"I know." Kairi's smile widened. "It's meant to do so."

"What are you talking about?" Dan exclaimed in terror.

"The Pyramid is the curse I have chosen to unleash onto an unsuspecting world." Kairi threw her arms out. "It all starts now. The end is near."

"We can't let you do that," Michael screamed. "We will not be part of it."

He turned to run toward the server but was stopped by a bullet in the back. He toppled forward and crashed onto the floor. Soha screamed, but was silenced by a bullet through her mouth. In the cascade of blood around him, Dan ducked forward, tackled the first guard, and crashed to the floor. Without knowing what he was doing, he tumbled forward and came to a standing position. With momentum on his side, he darted down the corridor. He could hear Kairi shouting orders to stop him, and felt bullets fly by his head, but he was familiar with the building and ducked into a smaller office.

He leaned against the wall, in the darkness, as the guards hurried past his hiding spot. He exhaled a sigh of relief when they didn't turn around.

CHAPTER EIGHT

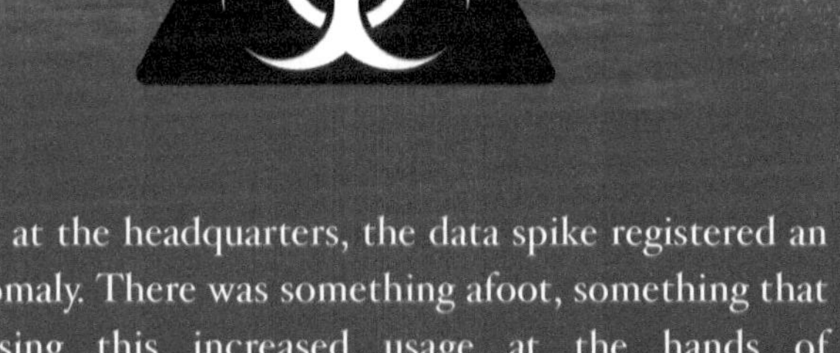

Back at the headquarters, the data spike registered an anomaly. There was something afoot, something that was causing this increased usage at the hands of consumers.

"Was the Pyramid properly disconnected?" Nick asked. They had requested for a shut down when the stats went through the roof, and no one seemed to be able to fix the problem.

"We were given a report confirming that it did, sir," Freya replied. "However, there were four emergency calls from the tech department. They lit up the switchboard, and Kairi herself went down to take care of it. They said they needed you down there, too."

Nick got up without saying a word and made his way there. The internal tech system was under renovation, but their offices looked like something out of a science fiction movie with minimalist, modern, sleek design. It was like taking a glimpse into the future.

"Mr. Harridan, we have an emergency," the chief in charge of tech said. "We tried to get the Pyramid offline, and it looked like it was working, but there are still some regions where the Pyramid is spreading rapidly." The man turned away from his computer screen and swiped through the red zoned regions throughout the country. "Though we are happy to see that the changes only occurred here and nowhere else."

"Thank you, Joshua. If there's no way to go offline in those regions, can we log everyone out instead?" Nick asked.

"Technically, yes," Joshua replied. "We tried that, but we got several password requests, and we were denied access. Apparently, no one in the department has those passwords or knows who put them there. We tried it already, which is why we had to go offline instead," replied Joshua. "But we don't know why that didn't work in the western areas."

"What do you suggest, then? What's our next course of action?" Nick asked.

Joshua went pale and looked down for a moment before looking back at Nick. He swallowed hard before replying, "We should go public, sir. People need to know what's going on; it's the only way to stop people from using the app without completely erasing the algorithm," Joshua replied. There was concern and fatigue in his voice when he finally spoke.

"What about erasing it geographically?" Nick suggested. "Can we get rid of it only in the affected area? Is that possible?"

Joshua thought for a second and typed a few codes into his computer before nodding profusely. "We can do that, sir," he replied with a bit of regained enthusiasm.

"Get on it, as quickly as possible," Nick ordered.

———

THAT AFTERNOON, KAIRI SAT IN HER ROOM, PONDERING the situation in her robe. She tied her hair in a bun and stared at the world outside of her window. She didn't want people to investigate what was transpiring. It was a loose end as it all started to unfold due to the memo she sent out. More importantly, the reputation and secrecy that Cabal had maintained for years was at stake. They could not afford to get exposed this way. Multiple ideas crossed her mind, just like the waves on a rough sea, one after another.

She already had blood on her hands after the encounter with the techs, but there was one big loose end: Dan. She needed him found and taken care of. Her thoughts raced until she made up her mind and rose to walk out onto the balcony. She let her robe fall open as she picked up her phone from the hidden pocket inside the sleeve. She looked at the screen as she scrolled through various numbers, until she found the one she was looking for. She put the phone to her ear as she let the soft breeze caress her skin the way it had toyed with the branches.

Cabal's survival as a secret organization was not only

due to luck. It was because several expert minds joined together under the single aim of achieving world domination. But not because they wanted to control everyone, like so many dictators before them. No, they were doing it for collective peace.

They naturally had to face countless situations, where people with certain skills were required. They had all kinds of specialists working for them. Cabal always kept these people on a tight leash so as not to let them run completely amuck. One of these dangerous people was Jackson, an investigator who had served as a detective in the NYPD. His cover as a private investigator earned him a living through consultations, but still, below the façade, he was deeply loyal and devoted to Cabal. A vessel waiting for it's time to serve its master.

"Jackson, it's Cabal's CEO speaking. You know the meeting place. I need to see you as soon as possible. I'll message you the meeting time."

Without waiting for an answer, she hung up and ordered her staff to ready the helicopter.

———

JACKSON WORE BLACK ATTIRE, DARK AS NIGHT, EXCEPT for the long black coat that had a line of white fur on the collar. From shoes to hat to sunglasses, everything was black. An attire that he associated with work, and something that meant he was in for business only.

Kairi's personal helicopter descended on Cabal's island. They landed on the helipad on top of the mansion, and Jackson approached the vehicle, staying a few paces away. While there, he reminisced about the time when Kairi was just another devotee that'd joined the ranks of Cabal under her father's wishes. Things had changed so much since then, and the girl she once was now had an entire island to herself, along with a mansion with personal guards.

Jackson was escorted to the guest room, where Kairi joined him. She sat down in a chair, her legs crossed, and her arms extended along the armrests. Jackson sat on the sofa and faced Kairi. She leaned to the side and produced a briefcase that she unceremoniously slid toward him.

"What is this about?" Jackson asked.

Kairi got up from her chair and faced the window, giving her back to him.

"That includes everything," she said curtly. "The memo that I sent, video recordings of every department from the past three days, and the project we're working on. You need to figure out how the virus got released without our order."

"Hm. I heard about the chaos," he said without emotion. "The information is spilling into the world. I guess you need to make sure that no one from the team snitches."

"That's why I called you. I need you to make sure no one's talking." She turned to him slightly. "And I'll take care of the rest."

———

THE BRIEFCASE CONTAINED RECORDED CCTV FOOTAGE of the members involved in the board meeting. Next to the tapes, there were files of all the members to whom the memo was sent. The files held personal information detailing origin, association, relationships, likes, dislikes, and other tedious and private information. He viewed the evidence on the footage and read the files extensively for hours.

In the end, he found a trail. The CCTV footage of the design room showed the artifact sitting in the machine, glowing eerily. The graphic designer had scanned the artifact in the top scanner and left the object there as he went to drink his coffee. At that moment, something had happened, a flash of light, and the screen had gone blank. The image flickered, and then the screen flashed on again; codes rained vertically down the screen in a steady glow, similar to the brightness of the artifact.

Jackson called over his assistant.

"Harry, can you fetch me all the files we have in Cabal's archives?"

"All of them, sir? There are quite a lot."

"Wait, you're right." Jackson raised his hand. "I'll come with you; it's better if we go to the actual archive. We might need to explore every single thread that links to this artifact."

———

AT THE ARCHIVES, HE MET KEENAN, THE MAN USUALLY in charge.

"I need to see all the files related to Cabal's artifacts," Jackson said to him.

"Hey, Jackson, sure thing. Long time no see," Keenan replied as he held out his hand for a shake.

Both men knew each other due to Jackson's regular visits. They shared greetings, and Keenan guided him to the back room.

"Where's Clarissa?" Jackson asked.

"I haven't seen her since yesterday," Keenan replied. "I

don't think she's feeling well; she looked sickly and pale. I sent her home, but I'm not sure what happened after that."

"There is something going around..." Jackson raised an eyebrow. "I hope she didn't catch it."

"They *have* pulled the lever, right?" Keenan asked.

"Yeah, but I think there's no stopping it anymore." Jackson sighed.

"I can feel this burden... Like the whole world will burn," Keenan said as his vision got a bit blurry, and a tear ran down his cheek. Not an overly sentimental man, but it still got to him.

Keenan always kept his eyes on Clarissa's Pyramid account and had seen her gradual transformation. But what he'd seen the day before was way worse than that. He really hoped it was a sickness, and not what was going on with the Pyramid, that was affecting Clarissa.

Jackson found the files on the artifacts, and after looking through them for a while, he discovered the origin of the anomaly. Found what he'd been looking for. With great efficiency, he managed to uncover the entire affair. After all, that was what he had been hired for.

The artifact was an old device that functioned when combined with an electrical charge. Once a charge was sent through the device or close to it, it was designed to emit a psychic impulse of addiction that influenced people's minds based on the instructions associated with the charge. It had the innate ability to reprogram a person completely. In a way, killing the brain, creating apathy and a great hunger for human flesh.

When the artifact had been scanned for the Pyramid's logo, the electrical charge initiated the device, which considered the memo to be the instructions, and carried out its designated release of the virus. The algorithm itself worked on the principle of electricity, and somehow, must've traveled through the Internet and into the entire online web.

Did this cause the massive anomaly in people's bodies? Jackson pondered.

After looking through the data, Jackson brought the information to Kairi. She was elated to know the cause of the outbreak. Kairi was convinced that this new information would lead to a solution. After all, that was how her whole life had worked: find the problem, fix it.

She was, unfortunately, blissfully unaware of how complicated and sensitive the situation had gotten.

"With this information," Kairi said to Kelly as she got her up to speed, "do you think we can do a laboratory assessment to see how effective our plan will be?"

"This will actually help us out," Kelly replied. "Also, Mr. Harridan called. He said that the Pyramid has properly shut down now, and they're extricating the virus. Hopefully, within a week, the Pyramid will start running again as before."

"Can you contact his secretary and bring me the details about everything he is doing?" Kairi asked.

"Sure, Ms. Kairi," Kelly replied. "Do you also want me to fetch the scientists for the lab test?"

"Yes, keep it a secret, and find me three suitable and reliable candidates, okay?" Kairi demanded as she watched Kelly get a little uncomfortable, but still agreed politely.

Cabal had come down hard on Kairi, wanting her to find some of the people affected by the virus so that they could perform their lab studies. It was vitally important to see the effects in a controlled environment to ensure that their motives were indeed accomplished. The subjects would be kept unconscious and in isolation. Kairi, eager to please Cabal and avoid them finding out what she was up to, headed to the lab with her guard and asked the scientists to prepare the rooms for their subjects.

The head doctor, a man named Christopher Wells, stood over a tablet, where flashes of various Pyramid images sped past his eyes.

"Can this facility be ready for test subjects within the hour?" Kairi asked once Dr. Wells turned around.

"It can." He nodded. "But we have already learned a lot from social media, and also from candid footage posted online."

"What do you mean?" Kairi asked.

"We can clearly see the effects of the virus on the mind after being unconscious for a brief time," he continued. "After prolonged exposure, it seems that the subjects have passed out. I believe the stress on the brain triggered it. You will notice that as they come to, the first thing they reached for was their phone to access the Pyramid app."

Kairi nodded. That was a high-level addiction. With every scroll the mindless subjects did, the worse they became.

"We already have two subjects," he said after a moment.

Kairi snapped to attention.

"You do?" She felt perturbed.

"Sure, we do." Dr. Wells looked at her. "They are right through there. Do you want to see them?"

Kairi nodded again, and he led her through a pair of heavy doors and down a hall.

"What happened with the two people brought in last time? The one with the gun wounds?" she asked casually as they walked down the hall.

"Both passed away; not much could be done. Don't worry, there's no trace of them," the Doctor explained. He had long been under Kairi's thumb, his pay too good for him to ask any questions.

"Good," was all Kairi said. Dead meant no loose ends, so it was one less thing to worry about.

They went through another set of heavy doors and entered a small observation room. Two young women were tied to boards attached to the wall. Their arms were free, and they both held onto a phone. They barely paid any attention to Kairi or Dr. Wells as they entered. Dr. Wells scribbled notes on his tablet with a finger, and then ordered an assistant to take away their phones.

Both became furious. They thrashed violently against the restraints with such furor that Dr. Wells feared they might pull the boards straight from the wall. The guard pulled out his gun and aimed it at the women as their yellow eyes peered at them, teeth gnashing violently. They were turning into monsters.

Wells held up the phones just out of reach from them, and they clawed the air in futile attempts to grab them. With every movement, they became angrier, their pale complexion covered in a sheen of sweat.

Kairi observed it all from the one-way mirror at the side of the room.

The two subjects acted in an irrational way and screamed for their phones to be given back to them, or at least, that must be what they were trying to do. All that they could vocalize was a guttural gargling that sounded like the ravenous snarls of rabid wolves. They didn't seem to care whether they were being studied in a lab or not, why they were restrained. There was no sadness in their eyes, only anger. They only dwelled on their phones, and they cried out for their devices; nothing else seemed to matter.

"You can see the extent of violence they possess." Wells looked at the mirror. "Look at her, she's hitting the wall in frustration. I will have no other choice than to give them their devices back, or they will destroy themselves."

"No, don't give them back; just see how far they'll go," ordered Kairi by pressing the call button behind the mirror.

"But they'll lose their minds if the phones aren't given to them," Wells tried to reason.

Kairi ignored his reply and decided that it was best to stay the course. She then asked the doctor to provide her with a complete analysis of the case.

"So, as far as we know, the virus affects people's choices by altering their preferences, and suggestibility by lowering their conscious resistance. In other words, it makes them numb, and then introduces a digital product as a drug to fill in that void of meaninglessness. In essence, rotting their brains while keeping their bodies active. This forces subjects to perceive the Pyramid as the reality of life and a meaningful entity," Dr. Wells spoke out loud as he continued to watch the subjects thrashing.

Kairi remained silent, but the voice inside her turned sinister at this news.

I want to see this on a larger scale, the little dark voice inside her head said. *I want control.*

Now, she knew the intentions of the virus and how it could be used in her cause, but it would have its consequences.

———

Cabal was used to developing intricate backup teams and plans. They even had plans in place for war — they controlled everything.

However, this incident was something wholly unplanned for them. Nick was not happy about the sudden update. Spontaneous chaos had high stake consequences since it was incredibly unpredictable. The sky-high usage of the app could have been their end if the world's governmental agencies started investigating this rupture. For once, Nick felt that Kairi had lost control.

"Mr. Harridan, may I come in?" Freya asked, poking her head in the door.

He looked up at her and felt a sudden urge to hug her, craving human contact.

"Yes, come in," he replied.

"Ms. Kairi sent you these files this morning," Freya said. "You weren't in the office, so I kept them safe." She handed him the sealed package.

"Thank you, Freya," he replied.

To his surprise, she just stood there and didn't leave.

"Is there something else you want to say?" He raised an eyebrow.

"Not particularly." She smiled at him. "But Kelly, Ms. Kairi's assistant, has been getting too comfortable with me. She asks about you a lot. Almost every conversation ends with you," Freya replied hesitantly. "I don't know what it means, but I thought you should know."

Kairi is keeping tabs on me now, Nick thought.

"Do let me know if anything else goes on, alright? You may leave now." Nick waved her away.

Nick opened the package, and a stack of papers spilled out of it. He glanced over the documents and was astonished to discover that they detailed the War of Rusziye and the artifact linked to its wreckage. Had her sister found another artifact? Or had she been hiding this all along? A pit of hatred grew in his heart. Was she going to release this virus to the public? That would be devastating!

In that instant, he thought about confronting her. It would be a big deal, and it would lead to open conflict. No, he needed to work in the shadows. Slowly, he began to devise his own plan. He would support her, yet silently undermine her work at every angle. He needed his own team. A team to serve justice.

———

"The Pyramid is up and running again," Dan said as he looked at the screens. He was sweating despite it not being cold, his nerves on end since what had happened the other night. But he knew being in plain sight and surrounded with people at all times was the best he could do. If he were to run, they'd find him. And after all, they said there was safety in numbers, and right there, he felt the safest.

"We had to work overtime to get the interface running again. We have pretty much rewritten the whole algorithm to get the virus out," Tara complained. "My back hurts from sitting so much. I think these were some of the most exhausting hours of my life."

Dan tried not to let a bitter laugh out at that. For him, it had certainly been exhausting. The secrets he was holding in were eating him up from the inside, and he couldn't remember the last time he had slept.

"What do you think the virus was? That they released?" Freya asked as she got closer to Tara.

"No one seems to know," replied Dan. "Even the

coders aren't aware of anything. We were only told that a computer virus had gotten into the system without our knowledge or approval, and that it had to be removed. The whole system was rebooted."

"Guys, I think I can figure it out...," Freya said abruptly. "We need to know what's going on, and I'm gonna find out."

She trusted herself a lot around computers and secrets, and if there was a secret that needed to be uncovered, she had to be the one to do it. She had to figure out what was going on with the Pyramid, and she had to take the whole place down. But she needed plans, strategies, and allies. She knew that much now, and she was starting to prod the closest people to her to see who she could trust.

"No way, don't get yourself involved in those things," Tara said, lowering her voice. "You just got the job. Keep a low profile, unless you want to disappear like Fatimah." Tara raised a warning finger, her whispers barely audible.

"Who's Fatimah, and what happened to her?" Freya asked.

"She was Nick Harridan's secretary. And somehow, one day, she simply disappeared. Nick was on a world tour, and she was just... gone," Dan explained to Freya.

"Oh," Freya said while looking at Nick, who was standing on the other side of the glass window inside his office.

"We can carry out our own research. We'll help you do this, but you need to be careful where you tangle yourself, okay?" Dan said.

They all looked at one another in silent agreement.

———

KAIRI ATTEMPTED TO CALL CLARISSA IN ORDER TO ASK her to retrieve everything they had on the second artifact that had recently got into her hands. The box had sat unopened in one of her security boxes for a while, but with everything going on, she thought it was time to pull another ace out of her sleeve. She sent her the picture of an exquisite black and red piece, but minutes passed, and Clarissa did not respond. So, she sent it to Keenan instead, hoping the man would be faster to reply.

"Oh, would you look at what Kairi just sent me," Keenan whispered as he sorted through the old testaments. "The Scartzest."

Keenan was puzzled when he looked at the picture, and it slowly dawned on him that the background of the image was indeed Kairi's office. The device was extremely powerful, a tool of pure manipulation and control. One that he thought had been lost for generations. How did she find it?

If Clarissa had been around, she would surely have known the answer, but she'd been gone for two days now — the only evidence of her existence on the Pyramid, which had resumed as soon as the app went back online.

He wasn't sure if getting those files to her was a good idea, but he was sure that Jackson had already been looking into them, along with the other artifact files. If he didn't go to her, she'd surely come to him, and what was he supposed to do? Hide the files? Reluctantly, he made his way to her office.

"Kairi, may I come in?" Keenan asked as he held the files in his shaky hands.

Kairi waved him inside, and Keenan saw the artifact lying on the center of the table. It was black with red stripes, and it looked eerily vibrant. Kairi stroked it carefully, imagining how much more harm it could cause.

"What do you have for me?" Kairi asked.

"It is an old book that describes almost all of the artifacts in detail," Keenan said. "It was buried deep down in the archives, and I only found it recently. It contains all the long-buried histories of the artifacts and their functions. It looks almost like a journal that someone put together, but it doesn't say who wrote it." He turned over to the page that described the one that glowed on the table.

"Scartzest, the Cyprus addiction," Keenan read. "The book states that it was made during the Hiatus period, the era of complete darkness and war.

"The Populus constructed artifacts as weapons of war to serve them for eternity, by making everyone addicted to a specifically targeted activity. It harnessed a strain of virus that was connected to the algorithmic power. In other words, it had an association with electrical charges, which was considered magic at the time. Not knowing how many artifacts like this they'd need, they created a few different ones, playing with the formula and getting better and better each time," Keenan explained.

"So, a weapon for control," Kairi said in a low voice.

She looked up briefly from the book, and then looked far away in the distance with a pondering mind.

"Yes, it is a master of manipulation and control," Keenan reconfirmed as his breath grew heavier.

"Do you think it can kill a person?" Kairi asked cryptically, but Keenan had no answer. He just blankly looked at Kairi, hoping that day wouldn't come.

———

THE LIGHTS FLICKERED IN THE OFFICE. FREYA WOKE UP from her slumber at the computer and instinctively checked the time on the screen. Midnight had struck once again, and she had been left alone inside the building. Everyone else from her team was long gone, but she had offered to stay late, with the excuse of making sure everything was okay. Instead, she'd been going through the Pyramid data and trying to find something helpful.

The monitor flickered in an eerie, erratic manner, reminding her of a horror movie as she tried to wake the computer back up.

She looked around the dark and empty office, and a shiver ran down her spine. It was as if the lights had all gone out at the same time; the only thing working was the flickering screen in front of her, bathing her face in a sickly white glow.

She scratched her head for a moment and waited, thinking she had just heard something amid the eerie silence. Suddenly, she heard the shuffling of feet in the corridor outside the room. Not normal shuffling, no, more like someone with a bad limp trying to make their way across the thick carpeted floor.

Freya slid back on her chair and turned around, just to see one of the office guards burst through the glass door, lunging at her. She cried out in terror as the snarling figure, skin rotting and falling off, came for her with arms stretched out. The sound of shattering glass was deafening as fragments rained all around the thing.

It must have broken several bones in its body as it came through the safety glass, but did not seem to care; instead, it came at her with fervor. She rolled to the side as a claw-like hand almost scratched her face. The thing couldn't stop itself as it missed her, and its head crashed right into her desk, breaking open its forehead.

Blood sprayed on her monitor as the thing that was once an officer moaned, twitched, then fell still.

"What the fuck?" Freya said aloud.

She moved closer to the body and poked at it. The flesh underneath the uniform felt squishy and damp. She moved back with a disgusted air. The creature looked very much like the images she had recently seen flashing across the Pyramid app.

Before she could consider it much longer, another moan emanated from the hallway. She looked back at the shattered door, only to see several more "things" coming for her. She needed to act quickly. She scrambled for her phone, but she couldn't find it. So instead, she gingerly slipped the gun out of the officer's holster.

She had some training with a firearm. She wasn't the best shot but could make it work. She checked the clip, and it was full. Sliding it back into the gun, she released the safety and decided to make her getaway. There was only one entrance to the office, and that was where five or six creatures were coming at her.

The shots made her ears ring as she fired at the first person coming at her, a woman she remembered seeing a few times at the reception desk. The first bullet went wide and hit the wall behind her. The second tore into a man next to her, creating a crater in his chest. He didn't flinch. As the receptionist closed in, Freya managed to fire one straight into her head as she screamed in terror.

An explosion of blood and brain matter showered the creatures behind her as she collapsed onto the floor. Freya realized that she couldn't keep up as they closed in on her. She needed to bolt.

She took a deep breath and darted toward the man with the hole in his chest, feeling the wetness of his mutilated torso as she crashed into him. He wheezed as she pushed him and fell against the others coming after. Snarls and dirty fingers came for her, but she dashed to the right, running for her life.

She glanced over her shoulder, only to find them running toward her. She fired at them, but it only seemed to antagonize them more.

She came to a crossing, and suddenly, bumped into someone coming around the corner. She stopped cold before even looking to see who, or what, it was, lifted the gun, and placed the barrel against their temple.

"Woah," Dan said and held up his hands. "What are you doing?"

"You can talk?" Freya seemed perplexed.

"Of course, I can talk," Dan replied. "Can you put down the gun? What the hell are you doing with that, anyway?"

Freya did so reluctantly, but she could tell from the hue of his skin that he hadn't yet turned into one of the ghouls.

"What the fuck is happening here?" Freya asked as she lowered the gun.

"What are you talking about? You're the one pointing a gun at me. I think I'm the one who gets to ask that question," Dan said worriedly. "What are you even doing here so late? I thought you left at the end of your shift."

"I could ask you the same, but there's no time for chit chat... Look at that!" Freya pointed to the group of creatures that were turning the corner at that very moment, her hand shaking as she did. She knew they'd be coming for her, and knew they didn't have much time. They needed to do something.

"Shit!" Dan cursed. "Follow me."

He grabbed her free hand and pulled her down the path he had just come from. Freya could hear the moans from the creatures as they came closer and got more agitated. Dan led her through twists and turns until they came to an elevator.

As if by pure luck, the large metal doors opened when he pressed the button. He pulled her inside, and they watched as the monstrous beings hurled their bodies toward them. The doors shut tight, catching an errant arm and snapping it in two.

"Can you please tell me what's going on?" Freya shouted as the elevator began moving.

"Calm down." Dan sounded too calm as he turned to her. "Let me just think for a moment."

He paced back and forth, and then hit the emergency stop button. The elevator jerked to a halt, and they scrambled to stay upright.

"Okay," Dan said. "What you saw out there... in the corridor..."

"Yeah?" Freya urged him.

"They're zombies." Dan watched her look at him with a skeptical air. "They were brought about by a virus that was sent through the Pyramid app when the outburst happened."

"What?" Freya was taken aback. "How is that even possible?" She knew the app was affecting people, but zombies? That was on a completely different level.

"Well, you see..." Dan took a deep breath. "There is this ancient organization called Cabal, which is deeply rooted inside the Pyramid. Most people think it's just a board of important people who give us money, but they're so much more than that. From what I've been investigating, it has existed since the first societies were formed. They have been an invisible hand, guiding and dominating the world's events behind the scenes. Apparently, there was an artifact that got integrated into the Pyramid's code, spreading a virus that reprogrammed people's brains."

"I don't get it." Freya just shook her head in disbelief.

"The code and algorithm infect the mind," Dan explained, "effectively killing the mind but allowing the body to continue living. The code drives the mind to want more of it, which forces the individual to go after whatever device has the Pyramid installed. Cabal isn't the group to blame here, though; it lies with someone else..."

"Kairi," was the only thing Freya could think to say.

CHAPTER NINE

Kairi patiently sat in her office, gazing out the window as the sun started to peak over the horizon. It was barely six in the morning, but she was ready to tackle the new day. The monitors on her desk showed images of zombies slowing down as light shone upon them. They shuffled through offices or collapsed against walls at the opposite side of the building, far enough not to be a worry for her.

She picked up the phone and called in Kelly, who had been instructed to stay at the office overnight in case anything unexpected were to happened. Kelly brought in the results of the subjects under investigation as Kairi instructed, dark circles under her eyes.

When Kelly brought the files, Kairi's heart raced slightly as she held them. The results showed signs of a complete mind shut down, and the hunger for the algorithm and human flesh dominated the charts. This was no different than what had been going on in their lives, constantly using the Pyramid, even while eating, walking, and resting. It was just elevated now and more intense. It was on a whole new scale.

Dr. Wells' research showed parallels between what the Pyramid had already done to what was going on now. The subjects had shown a very obvious obsession, where daily life revolved around the Pyramid, posts, captions, influencers, followers, daily feed, direct messages, and stories. In order to compete with others using the app, they shared forged and fake happiness on their profiles. In the end, they'd lost everything, including themselves.

Signs showed that they barely noticed anything outside of their phones. Refused to engage in any discussion that involved others. Had no subjective opinions or intellectual stimulation.

While Kairi read the results, she couldn't help but smile. The world was going through a phase that she had envisioned. The only thing that still made her nervous were the methods she needed to use to sustain this change. If it got out of hand, then there would be no way of controlling it.

She closed her eyes and thought logically about manipulating her way toward total control and domination. Her malevolent creation had worked faster than anticipated.

She called Kelly in again and asked her to arrange an emergency meeting with the director's board.

———

Kairi paced around the meeting room in excitement and met everyone with enthusiasm instead of her normal regal and disdainful air. As everyone passed through security and sat down around the conference table, she discussed the results and circumstances of the new update.

"We will be re-releasing the virus," she stated. "But this time, we have to make sure nothing gets out of hand."

She further proceeded to explain the procedure, looking at most of the directors looking back at her with almost blank stares. All of them had been instructed to download a staff version of the Pyramid upon entering the organization, making sure they were compliant enough to go along with her plan.

Before concluding the meeting, she told the members of the organization, "And be sure to keep this a secret. If word gets out, you better watch your back."

Only one of the members of the board brought up his concerns. Mr. Dickson, head of external affairs, told them all the story of a happy family he had known. One destroyed by the Pyramid.

"I hate to say this, Kairi," he said. "But they lived happily until this platform exposed them to the virus."

He paused and looked at the emotionless faces of everyone in the meeting room. He explained the statements from the parents regarding how their daughter behaved and what they did to help her out of the misery. Every day, she locked herself in her room, never bothered coming out, even for food, unless her mother forcefully dragged her out of the room. Mr. Dickson gave a long speech about what had happened, his eyes watering as he got to the more gruesome details.

After hearing the grim details about the victim, Kairi left the meeting without saying a single word, while Mr. Dickson stood there with the report in his hands. Everyone looked at one another in confusion and disarray, most of them unsure of how to feel about what was going on, a feeling of wrongness in the pit of their stomach, but resolution that they were doing what they were supposed to do.

Kairi stood in front of the elevator for a moment, taking it all in. It had been a breakthrough in her career to finally achieve what Cabal always wanted. But as she stood there, the misery suffered by humanity devalued the endgame. She thought about the ramifications of her ideals on the world. She tried to find a spike in her emotion, but she couldn't. There was no inner voice inside her, attempting to reason with her. Not a single word was coming to ignite remorse or guilt. There was nothing. She simply didn't have the ability to empathize with others.

When the heart was silent, and morality did not propose any disagreement, she smiled confidently and made her way back to the meeting.

As she opened the glass door, everyone went silent.

They were probably talking about me, Kairi thought. She stood upright and went on to declare complete control of the virus.

The men coughed and looked down at her plans, but Kairi knew she couldn't show weakness. If her authority waned, and her ability to control the virus was called into question, then they would pull strings to bring her down.

She needed them with clear enough heads to work for her, which meant control couldn't be total. But it was a gamble she'd been willing to take. Therefore, she proceeded with the advancement of her plan to transmit the virus at a higher speed. She told them about her intentions and what was required to mobilize the resources on a global scale. They questioned whether this could be carried out on a smaller scale for sustainability, and whether it was the right time to unleash the beast.

Kairi comforted them with facts and evidence using the recent case studies from Dr. Wells.

"What if we invest in businesses around the world?" Kairi explained. "In a way that still gives priority to the Pyramid? Let businesses know the market they should target based on who has the most followers on the Pyramid."

The idea was like a lightbulb in a sea of darkness. Indeed, there was no need for any further extension of the capitalistic reach of the Pyramid. A business was prone to death by its competition if it stopped changing, evolving, or expanding. All except two agreed, Flint Stone and Atlas Zayn.

Both men showed hesitation. "The Pyramid is everywhere. We're collecting data from every household, every structure, and every organization. Not only that, but we're also using this to develop economic schemes that are doubling our profit by millions. We are reaching the level of well-developed countries in terms of the money that we're making. Seeing all of this, do we really need another plan to double it?" Atlas argued.

Kairi kept a smile on her face, and her gaze on him. She felt furious inside as he challenged her authority. She wanted to antagonize him but knew she had to remain calm for the others in the room. Instead, she held a poll for whether this domination should take place or not. Naturally, everyone voted in favor of her plan, even those who showed resistance in accepting the idea, and just like that, the plan was set into motion.

The plan sprang into action soon after the meeting adjourned. All the startups and business ventures were called to join one large seminar. The Pyramid announced panels all around the world. Journalists and business advocates were invited. The latter were asked to join in the guise of "helping the brave entrepreneurs." It was advertised as another good deed by the Pyramid, another attempt to "aid" humanity. The seminars were set to be held in places where there was a high population and access to people. Among them were Mumbai, Berlin, Paris, Los Angeles, Milan, and New York City.

The seminars were going to be held on a larger scale and aimed for success. *How could they fail?* The world's most prosperous company aiding in a business, in return for one minor condition, was a no-brainer for anyone who had dreams and aspirations. Deals were drafted in bulks. People went home with uncontainable joy without realizing what they were getting themselves into.

THE LIGHTS OF HER MANSION IN SANTA CRUZ WERE dimly lit as Kairi enjoyed her success that night while sipping wine in her champagne-colored silk robe. The world had ended up precisely where she wanted it to. All her dreams were coming true. Soon, the world would be under her control.

In her loneliness, she imagined the entire plan

screened on her window. The whole world was suffering from this disease. The virus started infecting people and could be transferred from one person to another through bodily fluids.

Her thoughts were broken by the sound of a bell ringing. It was her security guard.

"Ms. Kairi, Jackson is here to see you," he said. "Should I send him in?"

"Yes, bring him to the lounge," Kairi replied. "I will be there in five."

Jackson walked up the steps leading to the beautiful mansion. A maid came into Kairi's chambers to inform her that he was waiting downstairs.

"Let him know I'm coming," Kairi told her. "In the meantime, offer him a drink."

She had been attracted to Jackson ever since she met him on her first case at Cabal, but she never dared to confess. Even though she wanted to at times, her ego refused to cross those boundaries.

However, it wasn't the only factor that stopped her. She was still in love with someone else.

She seductively came downstairs and moved toward him. He was stunned to see how beautiful she looked. He praised her confidence and strength. Even though he wanted to keep marveling at her beauty, the resistance and coldness radiating from Kairi stopped him. He always felt something surreal in their meetings; there was an intense desire for closeness.

Jackson never showed it, but he wanted his hands on her beautiful skin, to feel her cold pulse on his warmth. He watched as her lips moved while she spoke about destruction and control. Her hands were placed elegantly on her lap while she looked across the room in search of something, and the thought of simply giving her some warmth and comfort made him blush.

Instead, he felt obliged to penetrate through her thick and cold walls so that her heart relaxed. She had an egocentric personality that barely listened to or cared for anyone. She always did things that she thought were best rather than considering the opinions of others. After this raw desire, evident in their eye contact, Jackson brushed off the thought. He started discussing the important situation at hand.

A few days ago, she had ordered Jackson to conduct a secret investigation on those affected by the virus and where it all started.

As he conducted the investigation, he felt that there was strange behavior in one of her departments. That someone was doing something out of the ordinary, replacing files within the department. However, she refused to believe him; she knew she had the staff wrapped around her little finger.

"I know what I'm doing," Jackson retorted. "I've been doing this for decades." Feeling rejected and belittled, he walked out, leaving Kairi in her bubble all alone once again.

While Cabal enjoyed immense success, Dan and Freya started their own investigation and moved against the company. They exited the elevator once it reached the basement level the night before, full of renewed energy as they knew they had to do something about what was going on.

Getting off the elevator, Freya felt taken aback after

Dan's confession. From Cabal to the virus to the Pyramid. What the hell could she do now? If her conviction to bring down the social media giant had been strong before, it only grew stronger now.

As they stepped out into the concrete cave of the parking garage, they found themselves surrounded by dead bodies scattered everywhere. Dan wondered if it was the first time this had happened, or if the bodies would be cleared by morning as if nothing had happened. How was this all happening under their nose without them knowing?

"What now?" Freya felt dejected. She didn't know how much more she could take.

"These look like dead zombies," Dan said as he kicked one of the hideously deformed bodies softly with the tip of his shoe. "Someone must've taken them out. This is odd."

"Who would do that?" Freya asked, but was interrupted by a trio of figures detaching from the darkness.

They were all dressed in riot gear: black uniforms with bulletproof vests and heavy boots. Their heads were uncovered, revealing faces smudged with blood and human gore.

"Who are you?" Freya asked, bringing the gun out from behind her back.

"Take it easy," a blonde man said, holding out a gloved hand.

"Unless you're a mindless zombie, we're not here to hurt you," a dark male added.

They all had rifles slung across their torsos and police-style batons in their hands.

"We are the Scars," the third member, a brunette woman, said. She approached Freya and Dan, her hand extended. "My name is Scarlett, and these are my associates, Angel and Akuma."

"The Scars?" Dan asked.

"We are a secret organization designed to take down Cabal," Akuma replied. "This virus has given us the vehicle to do just that. This outbreak is not what we expected, but it's certainly giving us motive to move faster."

CHAPTER TEN

The memory was like a bucket of cold water as Freya disappeared into her mind for a moment.

Isn't it crazy how a simple device can change your entire life?, Freya thought while she observed her brother sitting idly in the corner, hunched over his phone. *The last generation had it so much better, peaceful lives centered around physical interactions, meeting soulmates while getting a coffee from the shop nearby, writing letters to express love. Living. Everything just disappeared when technology took over.*

"Don't you have anything better to do, Cyrus?" she

asked, but there was no response. "Hey, can you hear me?"

Her brother looked up and annoyingly said, "What do you want? Can't you see I'm busy?"

"Forget it." She spat while looking at her dry hands.

Everything had changed. She needed to do something about it. She had already lost her parents to divorce, and now, her only brother was addicted to a screen. She wanted to cry, scream, and put everything back to normal. She went to her room, sitting silently on the floor and touched her crucifix pendant. She had faith that she could make a difference with her new internship at the Pyramid.

Religion was no longer practiced in the world. Still, some hearts desired the comfort that the presence of God gave them. Freya knew that there was someone out there, and one day, help would come, and things would get better. She looked at herself in the mirror and thought: *Maybe I can be the help the world needs. Maybe I can change this world and make it a better place. But how? God, or anyone, if you're out there, and you're listening, then guide me.*

———

"Look at that!" Dan cried, pulling Freya out of her daze. "Is that a lizard?"

"Dude, are you afraid of lizards?" Akuma laughed as they bounced along the desert in Akuma's jeep.

Dan rolled his eyes. "No, I'm not afraid of lizards, but that one is huge! I'm just surprised."

He looked over his shoulder at the lizard sitting lazily on one of the big rocks they had passed.

"City people," Angel muttered under his breath as he stifled a laugh.

"So, tell us about the Scars," Freya cut in as her focus

returned. If she had an ally against the Pyramid and Cabal, she had to know as much as possible about them.

"We're an international group of trained fighters," Scarlett began from the passenger seat at the front. "The group first arose during the middle ages when Cabal first revealed itself."

"How did that happen?" Dan asked. "I thought the group was supposed to be a secret."

"It was during the war between the popes," Angel replied. "A huge rift in the Catholic Church occurred as Cabal tried to control the organization. Everything went haywire, and some of the mightier nations discovered the group's existence."

"What happened then?" Dan asked, leaning back to watch Angel better, who was sitting in the middle between him and Freya.

"Well, over the years, Cabal eradicated those nations and, once again, vanished into the shadows," Akuma chimed in from the driver's seat, his blond hair dancing in the wind. "A small group of European nations managed to escape, and thus, they created the Scars."

"We have been trying to bring down Cabal at every turn," Scarlett continued. "But they've just been too strong, too secretive, and ahead of us."

"Now they've messed up, though," Akuma said. "This virus they released was a fatal mistake."

"What are you going to do?" Freya asked.

"Oh, we've got a plan." Angel smiled and winked at her.

———

A WOMAN ENTERED THE OFFICE, LOOKING A LITTLE unsettled and pale. She was wearing a lot of makeup, but the dark circles were still visible under her eyes.

"Has Mr. Harridan arrived yet?" she asked.

"Hi. Um, no, I haven't seen him," Francesca said as she looked over her shoulder to the glass walls. She had taken over Freya's desk after she became Nick's secretary, moving over from the sales department. "What's up?" she asked the woman, but she just rushed into Nick's office. "You're welcome," muttered Francesca, looking at Tara.

Her friend was looking back at the door with her mouth open, a little nervous.

"What's wrong?" Francesca asked.

"Do you know who that is?" Tara replied with another question.

"No, I don't..."

"I should go check on her," Tara said as she stood up.

"I don't think that's a good idea. Did you see her eyes?" Francesca replied and turned back to her screen.

———

CLARISSA WALKED INTO THE OFFICE AND CLOSED THE door behind her without locking it. She'd be in and out. Her feet felt cold and heavy as she made her way carefully toward the desk. With shaking hands and a lump in her throat, she looked around to confirm that no one was coming, feeling like she was being watched.

She felt tired, and her pale skin was still falling off her face, barely concealed by the layers of makeup she had applied and the professional glue she'd used. Her mind felt muddled and tired, but there was one thing she was set on doing. She grabbed her phone; the desire to open the app was so strong within her, but she shook her head and didn't do it. She had to be stronger.

Slowly, she pulled out the last drawer, and under some files, she found the picture she'd been looking for. Clarissa hurriedly captured the picture on her phone and put the picture back inside the drawer, the phone back inside her pocket.

Suddenly, the door opened, and Clarissa jumped from behind the desk.

"What are you doing?" Tara asked suspiciously.

"Um... just leaving some files before Mr. Harridan comes in. He... asked me to bring them over from the archives." Clarissa walked past her toward the office door, and Tara stood to the side, letting her go.

"Hey, Clarissa?" the woman said before Clarissa could finish crossing the threshold, and Clarissa looked to the side, their eyes meeting for a moment. "Remember who your enemies and allies are, okay?"

Clarissa didn't know what to say. Was she calling her a traitor or a friend?

"I'll... fine. I'll be fine," she said softly, and she walked out the door. "We should both leave. Before Mr. Harridan comes in."

I need to find Fatimah, Clarissa thought as she opened her phone to look at Fatimah's picture. Those big and beautiful almond-shaped green eyes, with a chiseled face and long neck, stared back at her. She was beautiful. *I need to know what happened to her.*

She was about to jump into the elevator when the doors opened, revealing Nick inside. Clarissa halted, and there was an awkward moment of silence before the woman took a step back, and Nick finally smiled, his eyes sad and downcast to keep looking at her.

"Clarissa, come into my office, please," Nick said as he walked past and gently nudged her.

Through her haze and confusion, Clarissa could sense some tension. She wasn't sure what to do. She'd known Nick for years now, as she had been his first secretary while she was studying and before landing her position at the archives. She looked back to the elevator, and Nick looked at her over his shoulder, signaling for her to get moving. So, she did.

Nick ushered her in and went to sit behind his desk. "Close the door behind you," he ordered gently.

"Is everything alright?" she asked, standing by the door.

"No," he replied. "We are in a different realm now, aren't we?" he said thoughtfully. "One no one ever thought would ever become reality. I can't say much, but I wanted a minute with you. Be careful, okay? And if anything happens, you come talk to me. You know you can talk to me…"

He stood up and walked over to her, placing his hand on her shoulder gently. Clarissa could feel his warmth pass through her white satin shirt. His eyes were deep with concern. He wasn't just comforting her, but also warning her about the wickedness coming their way.

"Okay," she said.

Her mind felt worse than before. Whenever she was around Nick, her guard fell. It had been a long time since she'd run into him, with the building being so large, but at that moment, she just wanted to stay there. To be in his presence.

"Clarissa," Nick whispered as his hand fell from her shoulder. "I know the virus has gotten to you… but you need to fight it. I need you here and with a clear head. You're the smartest of us all, and I know I need you."

She tried to smile, but she couldn't remember how to.

Tara continued to kick her foot against the table, nervousness dripping from her face.

"Can you stop that?" Francesca begged.

"What's taking them so long?" Tara complained.

"Why do you care? Do you know that woman?"

"Of course," Tara explained. "That's Clarissa."

"*The* Clarissa?"

Tara blushed in response.

"Tara, if you like her that much, then you need to do something about it. The woman has no idea that you are drooling over her," she said. "And you've been mentioning her for weeks now. I'm sick of Clarissa this, Clarissa that."

Tara fell silent and looked back to Nick's office door. "I wanted to tell her, but we haven't spent much time together, and with the whole virus going around... I think she's got it," Tara choked out.

"I think so, too," Francesca agreed.

"Let's just drop it for now," Tara said, not wanting to think about her crush turning into a zombie before her eyes when she couldn't do anything about it. But maybe she could. Clarissa was one of the few rare cases of infected people who could still communicate and think, something they have seen around a bit. They called it the "slow strain," not sure if it was a different type of the virus, or it simply affected people differently. "What's the status of the Pyramid's interface?" Tara asked finally, getting back to work.

"I'm not sure; they're running some new tests and trying to relocate and compensate for all the losses," Francesca replied.

"This will sound totally off topic, but I'm sure that

Freya knows something we don't. We were supposed to investigate together, along with Dan, but she didn't show up to work this morning, and neither did Dan," Tara said. "Something's not right. Do you think something happened to them?"

"I don't know, but we gotta be careful."

Tara nodded and returned to her computer just as Clarissa came out of the office, her pale skin partially blushing red. Tara bit her lip, tried to come up with some words, and then watched Clarissa's back as she entered the elevator.

Maybe another day.

————

THE ARCHIVES WERE DUSTY, AS THEY ALWAYS WERE, when Clarissa came into the room. Keenan was piled high in old scent and papers.

"I think we should talk to someone about the information we've given to Kairi," Keenan said without looking up at her, as if he could feel her presence.

"You have a death wish?" she asked, putting her bag up on the table.

"Clarissa?" Keenan jumped up and groaned as he hit his head on a shelf. "You're back!" he added with a smile as he rubbed the sore spot. "I thought you were Tim, the new assistant. Oh my god, are you okay?"

Keenan told Clarissa everything that had happened in her absence, and she tried to listen as intently as her dizzy mind allowed her to. When he finished, Keenan looked worried, sweat trickling down his brow. "I think we need help; we need to tell someone what's going on. Maybe Jackson? He was here not too long ago."

"No, he works for Kairi," Clarissa said sternly. "But... maybe we can talk to Nick," Clarissa suggested.

"I don't know... but we need to speak up," Keenan replied while rubbing his forehead.

Clarissa put her hand on his and tried to comfort him.

"We'll be alright. No matter what, I will always be by your side."

Keenan looked at her, slowly leaned in, and hugged her.

"I won't leave you, either. I'm always here, with you," he whispered.

———

"So, your plan to end Cabal is to go to their headquarters and take them out?" Dan asked with a bewildered look on his face. He was expecting so much more from the Scars.

"What better way is there?" Angel asked. "Things are out of control, and we need brute force."

They had stopped at a large tent in the middle of the desert and picked up an army of riot gear clad figures. A cadre of European soldiers of fortune, all armed to the teeth. The base camp was set up not far from Cabal's secret headquarters.

"We've been watching Cabal for months," Scarlett said. "This is the perfect time to strike. Our inside intel tells us that they are ready to launch the next wave of zombies."

Freya looked at Dan, who shrugged.

"I guess this is as good an idea as anything," he said as the jeep bounced toward the headquarters.

A busload of soldiers followed in their wake.

CHAPTER ELEVEN

The jeep skidded to a halt in a cloud of dust in front of the black building, with its castle-like towers looming above them. A group of people had suddenly risen from the sand, and Akuma panicked. Freya and Dan yelped as the car came to an abrupt halt and nearly tipped over on its side.

The bus driver behind them had to hit the break hard to avoid ramming into them. The vehicle spun on its side, rolled, hit a dune, and then vaulted over. The group in the jeep screamed as the bus soared overhead and crashed on its side atop a mass of zombies trying to crawl free from the sand.

"It's a fucking trap," Angel yelled.

"They knew we were coming?" Dan asked.

"Sure, seems like it," Scarlett replied. "The sun is setting, and that means the zombies are more active."

"Go, go, go!" Akuma cried as he opened the driver's side door.

They all rolled out of the jeep, weapons raised. Angel tossed Dan a gun as they rounded the bus, its wheels still spinning in the air.

Scarlett and Akuma fired shots at the zombies still trying to emerge from the soft sand, sending brain chunks flying in the dusk.

Angel and Dan checked the bus, opening the doors in the back and helping battered and bruised troops out into the breezy evening air.

"How many are injured?" Angel asked.

"Not sure," a man replied from inside. "There are at least ten of us dead from the impact."

"Damn it!" Angel yelled. "Well, we need to advance before we lose any more time."

He gestured toward the black industrial building with its towers, and the survivors of the impact started to move out.

A mass of black clad troops rounded the bus. Small explosions erupted from the engine, lighting it partially on fire. Angel led the army, ordering them to take a knee and open fire on the zombies silently coming toward them. Freya noticed how they picked up speed as the sun continued to set, and the shadows from the towers grew longer. The Scars shot at the zombies, aiming for their heads, but the shots went wild as row upon row of growling ghouls came closer. Some of the Scars quivered in their boots and turned to run away.

"Hold the line," Akuma commanded as the Scars ran past him.

Suddenly, the large entrance to Cabal headquarters opened, and a line of soldiers — dressed in military wear and faces covered with cloth masks — appeared, automatic carbines held high.

"Shit," Scarlett whispered right before they opened fire.

The night air came alive with the crackling of gunfire. Several of the Scars fell while the zombies came upon them and devoured their bodies.

"Hold the lines, you bastards," Akuma continued, but the line broke.

The Cabal troops advanced at a slow and deliberate pace, taking out the Scars one by one; the rest scattered and ran off.

A stray bullet caught Akuma in the shoulder. He fell onto one knee, but Angel caught him.

"We need to get out of here," Scarlett told Dan and Freya, who were hiding behind the bus. "Follow me."

Angel jumped into the driver's seat of the jeep, kicking and flailing at zombies as they fell toward him.

"Get inside," he demanded, and the others did as they were told.

Bullets bounced off the vehicle as it sped off. Several Cabal jeeps followed, turrets armed with machine guns firing in their wake.

"We need to find refuge," Scarlett screamed while firing out the back.

"There is an old ghost town up ahead," Akuma panted, clutching the wound in his shoulder.

"Then head for it," Scarlett demanded.

Angel sped up, weaving left and right to avoid the bullets from the jeeps following them.

"Turn off the headlights," Dan said. "The sun has set, and they won't be able to see us in the dark."

Angel did as told, and they abruptly vanished into the desert.

THE MORNING FELT ECSTATIC. KAIRI HAD GATHERED ALL the relevant information from her recent experiments. It was only a few days before she was finally going to release the virus globally.

"I feel powerful," Kairi said to Silvia as she was getting ready for the day.

"Well, Ms. Kairi, you worked and sacrificed a lot to get here. I'm sure it will be worth it in the end," replied Silvia as she combed through Kairi's hair.

"There is still a lot more to finish, but I think, in the end, we will dominate the world. It was always my dream to ignite terror, and I think I'm closer than ever," Kairi confided in her. "I just have to make sure no one gets in my way."

Silvia didn't reply; she just nodded and went to get her jewelry.

"Do you want to wear diamonds today?" Silvia asked, picking up an elegant necklace with a little oval diamond in the center.

"No, give me the ruby necklace. I want to feel powerful and..."

"Unstoppable?" Silvia finished the sentence.

Kairi smiled at her and nodded. "Today is the day. Can

you ask Henry to arrange a board meeting?"

"Sure, Ms. Kairi," Silvia replied and dismissed herself.

There was complete silence in the room. Kairi looked at her reflection but felt nothing. There was no emotion left in her.

———

Henry brought everyone from Cabal's team together, the elite personnel, the investors, and the sole originators. People gathered at Cabal's private island in the Atlantic Ocean, a place originated to keep all of Cabal's affairs hidden. Kairi's private jet landed on the central port of the island, and she took the secret entrance at the back, making her way into the hidden mansion.

The mansion was enormous and surrounded by thick forestry. The depth and use of a magnetic field around the island protected the place from being identified through satellite imagery. Even when crusaders embarked on a mission or cargo ships voyaged, no one noticed the island. It was completely concealed.

"Has everyone arrived?" Kairi asked.

"Yes, for a few hours now. They are relaxing in the meeting room. Dinner was served a little while ago."

"There's no time for fun," Kairi replied sternly. "I wonder what it would take to get them motivated, stupid humans." Kairi scoffed.

"Do you think you're changing?" Henry asked out of curiosity.

Something has changed. This impulsive pull toward disaster is suffocating me, but I am unable to see through it. Kairi wanted to scream out the frustration she felt inside. The dilemma of ruining others while the guilt engulfed her was too powerful now to just disappear with a snap of two fingers. The artifact had done its work; soon, there will be an explosion. But no, she felt nothing, she told herself. Nothing at all.

"No, I don't think so. I'm perfectly fine," Kairi replied vaguely.

"Shall I escort you, then?" Henry offered his hand, and Kairi grabbed it.

The door to the meeting room opened, and cold air mixed with cologne hit Kairi's face. The men and women were seated around the huge oval conference table. They got up as Kairi entered and went to the podium.

"Good afternoon, everyone," she greeted. "I hope you're all in good spirits."

They nodded, and some even responded with a "yes."

"Good to know. You must be wondering why this meeting has been called with such urgency. To brief you on the matter, we have hit a breakthrough. After today, Cabal will finally reach its peak. There is something that I have been working on for months now. Though there have been some downfalls, I can give you full assurance that from today onward, we will only see progress." Kairi moved over to sit at the head of the table after the opening speech, and the meeting's signing sheet was passed around the table.

After everyone signed their name, Henry took their fingerprints to bind the seal of an envelope that would expose them all in case anything were to go wrong.

"Are we not going to discuss the attack on Cabal last night?" one of the senior members asked after a moment.

"What is there to discuss?" Henry asked. "The threat was dealt with, and the attackers dealt with."

"Don't you think the Scars finding the base indicates

that they're closing in?" the man continued.

"Not at all," Henry reiterated. "We are several steps ahead of them at all times. There is no way they can break us. Now, let's get back to business."

"Can you bring over the boxes?" Kairi asked, and Henry nodded.

"What boxes?" Habib questioned. "Why does it feel like you're going to ruin us?"

"Trust me, this is nothing compared to the harm you have done to humanity. We all know your, let's say, extracurricular activities," Kairi replied.

"Are you blackmailing me?" he asked, slamming his hands on the table.

"No, of course not." Kairi grinned.

Henry soon walked back into the room, holding two black concealed boxes. He unlocked them and stood beside them with the keys.

"These boxes contain artifacts that, as you may know, have been gathered by Cabal over the years. However, what we have all been ignorant of is the fact that these artifacts contain powers," said Kairi, hearing murmurs in the room. "The sort of powers that can change the world."

Habib coughed and cleared his throat loudly.

"Habib, is there something you want to say?" Kairi asked. "Something bothering you?"

He shook his head, fidgeting his fingers on his lap and avoiding eye contact.

Kairi slowly turned her head away and proceeded to show the artifacts. Everyone was stunned. There were gasps and whispers in the background. The room went silent as the golden crimson light emerged from her left hand, and blue neon glowed from her right hand.

"These devices were programmed to administer domination. Back in the day, a group of individuals developed these artifacts to conceal the sheer reality of the dark world," Kairi said.

"What do these devices do?" Flint asked.

"This red-striped one emanating a neon glow is called Scartzest. It was the product of the Hiatus period," Kairi explained.

"The period of infamous torture and rebellion," added Henry.

"Yes. They used this device to turn people into slaves during the War of Rusziye," continued Kairi.

"No way! Is this the same device that trapped the devil?" asked Flint as he moved across the table toward the artifact.

"Yes, as per the records," replied Kairi.

"What are you suggesting, Kairi? Do you want us to release these to the public?" Habib asked. Silence lingered in the room as his words echoed. "Do you know how much damage this will cause? This will ruin the entire system, and God only knows what will happen if this gets out of hand."

"Where is Nick Harridan?" asked Atlas, jumping into the conversation. "Shouldn't he be here?

"Why would he be here, Atlas? It's not like Kairi's going to let anyone get in her way," Habib chimed in. "We're just her pawns, and Kairi knows Nick doesn't agree with her methods."

"Enough!" Kairi took a deep breath, and then lowered her voice. "Habib, if you don't want to be a part of Cabal, then you are free to leave." Kairi turned to Atlas. "And Atlas, it's better that you leave Nick out of this."

"What's the point of this meeting, then?" Flint asked.

"I want to better understand and explore these artifacts. I think we can use them to our advantage and shape the world," replied Kairi.

"Also, we're here to take a vote," Henry added as he followed Kairi's orders. "Those who support the decision to release the virus, stay in the room. Everyone else can leave." Henry opened the door.

"Yeah, got it, Henry. This isn't a vote; this is blackmail."

"Is it, Habib?"

Kairi stared at him, keeping her cool as the man got up from his seat.

And then she watched as Habib and three others picked up their things and left the room, leaving only six remaining.

She knew they wouldn't get far; they'd be dealt with as per her order as soon as they took one foot out of the mansion. Those men wouldn't ever leave the island.

———

DAN, FREYA, AND THE THREE REMAINING SCARS FOUND an old derelict building. They broke into it after hiding the jeep under a dirty old tarp to make sure the Cabal soldiers wouldn't find them in the dark.

"We'll stand guard," Angel told them. "You settle down for the night. We'll probably be here for a while."

Dan and Freya found a staircase that led to a basement. Dan suggested that they hide in there so it would be more difficult to find them in case Cabal invaded. Freya agreed and followed him into the dark. Surprisingly, they found a nurse's station among the labyrinthine corridors.

"What do you think this used to be?" Freya moved over to a gurney standing off to one wall.

"Some kind of business," Dan replied. "Lots of them have nurse's stations like this, but as to what happened here... It's anyone's guess."

Freya felt an overwhelming sense of dread wash over her, and she began to shiver. Suddenly, she broke down in tears, sobbing uncontrollably.

"What's wrong?" Dan put his hands on her trembling shoulders and cradled her to him.

"This is just too much." She turned toward him, her face leveled with his chest. "Cabal, the Pyramid, the virus. I had a dream of bringing the company to its knees because of the horror social media inflicts on society, but this is nothing like what I'd expected. This is so much bigger than us."

"I knew you had second intentions when you joined the business, but taking them down, really? On your own?" Dan tried to joke with her and lighten the mood.

"I was naive, okay?" Freya calmed down a bit as laughter escaped her, and she moved a bit farther from Dan. "I don't know if I can fight this anymore."

"We can do it together." Dan ran his thumb under her eye, wiping away a single tear. "I will be here for you."

She moved closer to him, and he moved his thumb to her chin, leaning in for a kiss but hesitated a moment. So much had happened in the last few days and hours, and Dan had been infatuated with her for so long, but he wasn't sure if Freya felt the same. Wasn't sure if she felt anything at all. Freya stood still for a moment, and then moved to her toes, leaning in and meeting his lips.

Time stopped as they kissed, hands embracing one another. The stress of the moment was wiped away for at least a few moments as they lost themselves in each other, not sure if they'd live much longer after that night.

CHAPTER TWELVE

"The zombies! They found us!" Akuma yelled as he looked out one of the windows.

"We're trapped!" Scarlett fired a couple of shots into the night.

"As far as I know, zombies usually can't climb," Angel said. "If we can get to the roof of this building, we can lure them toward us, and then take them out from above, one by one."

"Good idea," Akuma said. "Barricade the entrance, and then we climb."

The other two Scars nodded in agreement.

———

EVERY YEAR ON OCTOBER 19TH, NICK HARRIDAN visited the hilltop forestry. He would stay there for hours and hours, staring out into the horizon. This date held a special place in his heart. It was the date he not only met the love of his life, but lost her, too.

Fatimah Malik was someone who went out of her way to fight for justice and find solace. She met Nick on a plantation farm, one where a group of elite individuals took a few hours out of their busy schedules to help reduce climate change. They planted around ten thousand trees that day. Nick was still a student at the time, same as her.

"Hi, can you help me with this?" Nick asked as he sat beside Fatimah on the ground. "I seem to have fat fingers, and can't really grab the seeds without throwing at least a hundred of them in at a time."

Fatimah laughed and bent down next to him to help. As they dug up the soil and dropped in the seeds, their hands touched. And instantly, Nick was attached.

From that day on, Nick wanted to spend every day with her, waiting for her on campus, her apartment, and even when she worked at the coffeehouse. Over the course of two years, they were inseparable, traveling across the continental United States together and making love under the stars.

However, the world had other plans for them. Fatimah learned about Cabal, and when she did, she asked to become a part of it. Nick tried his best to convince Kairi and the other Cabal associates to welcome Fatimah as their own, but no one would.

Kairi knew that having Fatimah at the company would ruin Nick's focus. She could see her brother falling in love and growing weak. Love and power don't go together. There is always a choice and a sacrifice.

Three years ago, he was asked to make a choice between Fatimah and Cabal, and he chose her, Fatimah Malik.

Only to find her dead the next day.

Due to the lack of evidence, the case went cold, and no one bothered to further investigate the cause of death. The public never really found much about the death, all kept hushed, thanks to Cabal's influence. Unable to recover from the loss, he had to take a step back, which he was sure was the reason Kairi had been given the position that'd been rightfully his.

She'd been sitting in that seat ever since.

Nick had lost everything that was important to him. He confronted Kairi about it, but she denied any involvement in Fatimah's death.

"I'm sorry, Nick. But everything happens for a reason, right?"

And as sincere as Kairi tried to sound, Nick could see right past her. He eventually joined the Pyramid and became one of Cabal's advocates. He knew he had to keep a close eye on Kairi. He didn't trust her, and he wanted revenge.

———

A KNOCK WAS HEARD ON CLARISSA'S FRONT DOOR. She'd recently moved out from her parents' home and into her own condo. She looked through the peephole and saw Nick, looking slightly intoxicated. She quickly threw a cardigan over her shoulders and opened the door.

"Mr. Harridan, what are you doing here?" she asked as he moved past her into the living room. "Hey, are you okay?"

"No, I'm not okay. I have never been okay, not since she died. You remind me of her, a lot. The way you pour your eyes into mine, the way your lips move when your voice touches my ears. There is something in you that is just like her." He titled his head and looked at her while she sat there with her mouth open and her hand on his arm.

"Sir, I don't know what you're talking about," she replied.

"I know you are looking into Fatimah; I know you went through my things, and I want you to know that I'm not mad because, I guess, you care about me enough to look into my past," he muttered. "Also, just call me Nick."

"But, Nick...," she murmured as he grabbed her hand.

"Just tell me this, did you ever feel anything toward me?" he asked. "Did you ever like me?"

The desperation in his voice shattered her walls; her heart raced as her hand touched his face. She slowly moved her hand through his ruffled hair and looked into his eyes.

"I do like you; maybe I always did," she answered while he held her hand and kissed the tips of her cold fingers.

"Good, so it's not just me." He closed his eyes in comfort and wrapped his arms around her waist, pulling her closer.

Clarissa didn't push him away. He rubbed his hand behind her back as she gently moved her hands over his arms and shoulders.

"You're drunk. You might end up regretting this later, or you might hate me in the morning," Clarissa said.

"I'm fine, and I won't regret this later, and I will never hate you," he replied, bringing his face closer to hers. They were an inch apart.

"I'm not her, Nick. What if you only want this because I remind you of her?" she asked as she moved away from his embrace.

"I love her, always will, but that doesn't mean I can't be happy again. She taught me how to love, so that I can love again. And I do love you, Clarissa. You do remind me of her, but I am fully and consciously aware that you are not her. You are Clarissa, even if you *are* sick. And I want to help you."

"You really want this?" she asked as she heavily breathed under his embrace.

"More than ever," he exhaled into her neck and took off her cardigan; his warm fingers made her gasp.

Slowly, he kissed her neck, her cheeks, forehead, and lastly, her lips. Clarissa just couldn't let go of the softness his lips left on hers, and she kept wanting more. They collided like two long lost souls aching for one another. It felt unreal, magical, and too powerful to end.

———

Angel, Scarlett, and Akuma found a staircase leading them to the roof. They looked down at the swarm of zombies below as they attempted to burst through the entrance.

Angel placed his rifle on the edge of the rooftop and squeezed off a few shots. The sound of gunfire alerted the zombies below, who looked up at them. They snarled with fury, turned to the building wall, and began to scale it.

"Fuck, they *can* climb," Scarlett whispered. "I thought you said they couldn't!"

"I guess these zombies are different from the ones in the movies," Akuma said apologetically.

Suddenly, they noticed several rough hands grip the edge of the roof, followed by the snarling maws of rotten faces. The unmistakable smell of rotten flesh wafted toward them.

"They're all around us," Angel cried out and blasted the head of one of the zombies on his side.

"Just fire," Scarlett yelled back. "We have to get away."

Akuma picked up his rifle and shot in all directions while he screamed. Zombie after zombie went down as the bullets tore into their heads. Some were simply caught in the chest or shoulder, and continued to move toward them.

Angel moved closer to the edge, only to be grabbed by chapped and cracked fingernails. He cried out and emptied his clip as they pulled him down from the rooftop. He was overpowered by the swarm of zombies. Their teeth dug into his body, bit through the protective vest, and into his neck. Scarlett tried to save him, but it was too late.

Meanwhile, the zombies on the other side crawled over and overpowered Akuma. He screamed in pain as they swarmed him.

"Get out of here," he called to Scarlett. "Save yourself!"

Scarlett turned, tears in her eyes, only to see zombies all around her. Their yellow eyes staring at her, and their sinewy hands stretched toward her body. She was surrounded on all sides, outnumbered by tenfold.

"Shit," she whispered.

CHAPTER THIRTEEN

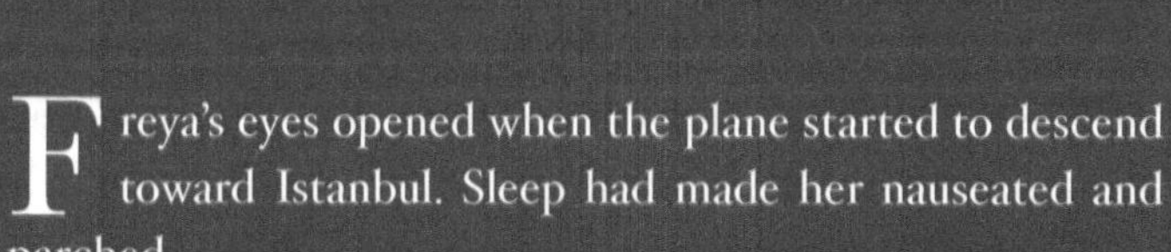

Freya's eyes opened when the plane started to descend toward Istanbul. Sleep had made her nauseated and parched.

"Can I get some water?" she asked the flight attendant.

"Sure thing, hot or cold?" the woman asked.

"Hot, please," Freya replied.

The weather was getting colder. She looked out the tiny window; the clouds were dark but felt comforting. There were lights glowing everywhere, like glittering stars of the land. Bright, and yet so far away.

She unbuckled her belt and went to wash her face. When she came back, she was welcomed by the attendant with her water and a bar of chocolate.

"Here you go," said the attendant with a smile.

"Thank you."

The plane soon descended further and further, and Freya packed up her belongings in her bag as she adjusted her belt and sat up straight.

People were hustling throughout the plane. Everyone gathered themselves as it went around toward the runway. Freya leaned against the window and saw the Galata Tower; she'd always wanted to visit it.

Freya didn't have many memories from her early years. She did remember feeling alone, many different houses that changed faster than her underwear, and then the Moores. The moment it had all changed. She'd been told her mother had passed away giving birth, and she had never known who her father was. And even though the Moores took great care of her, she often felt alone, and she had been looking for her biological family ever since she left school. It had taken her some long months to find a lead that seemed promising, so here she was. Trying to fill an empty space was impossible, but still, maybe these answers could give her some kind of closure on who she was.

Growing up, she barely made any friends due to her fear of abandonment, and she never stopped looking for something, or rather, for someone, someone who would be by her side no matter what.

Why are the Moores not enough? a voice whispered in her head, but she shook it off.

———

Dan and Freya listened to the gunfire echo throughout the building.

"We need to get out of here," Freya shouted as she heard the screams of the other Scars falling victim to the ghouls.

"We can't just leave them," Dan shouted back. "We have to help them!"

"I think it might be a little late for that. We have to leave, now! Head to Cabal ourselves!"

"Are you sure?" Dan asked.

Freya nodded. "The Scars aren't the only ones who need revenge. I'm taking down Kairi, if it's the last thing I do."

———

The passengers were told to remain seated until the sign to undo their seat belt was shown. Freya raised her head to see whether the doors had opened. Clutching her bag as it hung over her shoulders, it was almost like she was ready to run a race. The doors opened, and the passengers walked off the plane.

Once they reached immigration, a woman turned her phone on in front of her. Freya observed her boldness and sharp choice of clothing and makeup as the woman held it out and started taking pictures of herself. Everyone else in line was getting impatient. People asked her to move, but the woman just stood there, numb.

"What's wrong with her?" a man asked.

"Probably a social media addict. Don't you know what's happening in the United States? Everyone is slowly going insane," replied a woman who was holding her daughter's hand.

The immigration officer stamped Freya's passport, and she walked ahead, holding her bag and feeling full of energy.

She made a quick stop at a convenience store to pick up a new charger. People were walking up and down the aisles but with their camera open, taking pictures of the products and posting them online.

"Everyone is obsessed with their phones," Freya muttered.

"Yeah, it's difficult to find someone nowadays who doesn't care about the Pyramid," someone replied. "Name's Erik. Erik Holden."

"Hi, Erik. I'm Freya. Freya Moore," she replied. "What brings you to Turkey?"

"Oh, I'm part Turkish. My mom is Turkish and German, while my father is Korean but lives in Italy. It's a weird mix," Erik said as he walked with her through the aisles. "What about you?"

"I was born in the States, but I... I'm here to visit my uncle. I think he lives here."

"Think? Well, I'm quite the regular here. Care for a travel buddy? Traveling alone can be quite dangerous, especially for women," Erik offered.

"And how do I know I can trust you?"

"True that, but it also looks like you're capable of beating me up."

Freya laughed. "I *have* taken a self-defense class or two in the past."

She walked down another aisle and came across an array of Turkish desserts. "Alright, travel buddy, I'm starving. What do you recommend? I'm thinking Turkish Delights?"

But Erik shook his head. "Nah, go for the baklava. Way better. The delights are overrated."

As Freya walked up to the counter to pay, she noticed that even the cashier was hooked on the app. Rolling her eyes, she inserted her card and turned back to Erik.

"So, where are you staying?" Erik asked.

Freya shrugged. "Probably a hotel. I haven't decided yet. I'm usually a last-minute type of person."

"I have an extra room at my mother's place. It's usually empty. You're free to crash if you want."

"Trying to kidnap me?"

"Nah." Erik waved his hand. "Just thought I'd offer. But here." He pulled out a piece of paper and scribbled on it. "Here's my number and the address, in case you change your mind."

"Thanks, I'll think about it."

"Listen, I should really get going, but it was nice meeting you, Freya. I'll see you around!" He waved goodbye and walked away.

Freya felt a rush of loneliness when he walked away, but it wasn't something she wasn't used to. She went to pick up her luggage and walked out to grab a taxi, the foreign air welcoming her into the city. As she looked outside the taxi window, more and more people were on their phones, scrolling through the app. When the car came to a stop, Freya watched as a woman crossed the street, staring at her phone without watching where she was going. Suddenly, loud squeaks were heard, people shouting left and right, and the woman was hit by a car.

Shocked, Freya didn't understand where the world was headed. People were dying, losing their sanity over social media. What was going on? What's happening to the world?

After a short drive, she found a hotel and booked a room. When she walked in, she immediately collapsed onto the bed. She dug into her pocket and pulled out the paper Erik had given her. She contemplated whether she should call him. He definitely *was* cute, and she wouldn't mind spending a day with him.

———

THE ZOMBIES CRAWLED UP THE SIDE OF THE BUILDING AS Dan and Freya snuck outside. They could see several bodies around the base. Quietly, they pulled the tarp off from the jeep and got in. Angel had left the keys in the car in case anything happened to him. *Smart.* Dan smiled at Freya, started the engine, and drove toward the black building.

———

THE NEXT MORNING WELCOMED HER WITH RAYS OF SUN hugging her. She woke up and called room service for breakfast. The hotel was extravagant with a high beige ceiling and a chandelier above her bed. The door knocked after half an hour, and a hotel staff member brought her the perfect Turkish breakfast. She delightfully indulged in the food as the warm bath was running in the background. She brought her morning coffee into the tub and relaxed as the water and bubbles floated around her.

An hour later, she dried herself off, threw on a pair of jeans and a white T-shirt, and grabbed her phone before heading out. Everyone she passed was heavily immersed in their phones as she made her way to the elevator, all scrolling through the Pyramid app.

When she walked out the main door, she stood still for a moment as the sun rays bathed her skin, the complete opposite of the chilly winter she dealt with back home. She then continued down the street, turned the corner, and out of the corner of her eye, she spotted a woman, crossing the road while on her phone. The memory of the other woman flashed before her eyes, and she ran down the street and grabbed her by the arm.

"Stop!" she screamed, pulling her away right before a car whizzed by.

"Oh my god, thank you so much! You just saved my life." The woman thanked her and walked the opposite direction.

"For now, anyway," Freya muttered behind her.

———

DAN AND FREYA WAITED OUTSIDE THE BUILDING AS CARS went in and out. The movements of Cabal made it difficult to break in without being noticed, so they decided to wait until it was dark. If they could avoid the zombies, who now silently shuffled around in the desert, they would be in the clear.

Dan had monitored the movements of the Pyramid employees through his phone. Something all high-ranking employees could do. He'd found out that Kairi was on her way to the building for a meeting, and they knew they had to find her.

"We need a key card to get inside," Freya said.

"What about that guy over there?" Dan pointed to a zombie dressed in the uniform of a Cabal soldier. "I bet you he has one hanging from his belt."

"Guess there's no harm in checking." Freya grabbed the gun from Dan and exited the jeep.

The sun was setting again, so she had to hurry. She quickly approached the docile creature and cracked it over the head with the butt of the gun. The zombie went down, and Freya rifled through the pockets. She found what she was looking for and waved the key card in the air as a sign to Dan that he could come out.

"Let's take the back entrance," she said as he came over. "It'll be less guarded, and we'll have a better chance of not being seen."

He nodded, and they quickly moved to the back of the building, snaking past shuffling zombies who were beginning to wake up.

Freya swiped the card over the reader, and it made a noise before the door swung open. They stepped inside.

"Where do we find her?" she asked.

"There must be a boardroom or something," Dan replied. "If she's anywhere, it would be there."

"Top floor?" Freya asked with a smile as she pointed to the elevator door right beside them.

Dan nodded and hit the button. They stepped inside and rode the elevator to the top floor. Freya was surprised that no one stopped them along the way. They were all either hiding or had turned. When they exited, they found a room completely surrounded by glass. And through it, they could see Kairi Harridan, dressed in a black suit and standing next to a man.

"You don't have to come if you don't want to," Freya spun around and told Dan.

"Wherever you go, I go." Dan smiled and kissed her on the cheek.

"Well, then," Freya said and pulled out her gun. "Let's end this."

She kicked down the door and fired. The bullet missed Kairi, but hit the man in the neck, sending blood across the board table.

"What the hell is this?" Kairi asked, raising her arms.

"This is the end, Kairi," Freya replied and aimed the gun at her. "You have ruined enough lives, and I will not let you do it anymore. I am shutting down the Pyramid, the virus, and everything you have ever built."

"You fool." Kairi smirked. "The wheels are already in motion. There is nothing you can do."

"Wrong," Freya replied. "If I kill you, then I can convince the company to shut it down. Nick is against you, so he'll do as I say."

Kairi smirked. "Go ahead, then. Hope you don't miss."

She hit a button on the table, and suddenly, a door in the wall swung open. A large monstrous figure bowled out of the little closet it had been hiding in. The action startled Freya, and her shot aimed at Kairi missed.

"Midnight is here." Kairi laughed. "I'd like you to meet my newest creation, the next step in the virus. An all-powerful creature that obeys my every word. And let me tell you, he's hungry."

Freya fired at it, but with no luck. The bullets simply sunk into the rotten flesh of the seven-foot behemoth coming toward her. It crashed right through the conference table. Dan grabbed Freya's arm and dragged her out of the room.

"We need to leave," he cried. "That thing is too powerful."

They ran through the corridor, the creature chasing after them, faster than any of the other zombies they had encountered before. They took the stairs this time, two at a time, listening to the footfalls of the creature closing in. As they landed on the first floor, they encountered a few soldiers but pushed past them. They listened to them scream as the creature tore through them.

Pushing through the back door, they found themselves face-to-face with a swarm of zombies.

"They've multiplied!" Dan shouted to Freya. "It's impossible for us to escape."

"We have to go back and find another way," Freya agreed.

They turned around and headed back in, only to be confronted by the creature once again. It stared at them, covered in blood and human remains. It snarled and let out a guttural howl. Freya shot straight into its head, but the creature simply shook it off.

It pounced at her, but Dan pushed her to the side, and she toppled. She screamed as she watched the large, pale creature sink its teeth into Dan's neck, nearly snapping his head off. His dying eyes looked straight at her as his head sprawled back and forth, pleading for her to run.

He didn't sacrifice himself for me to die here, she thought.

With tears in her eyes, she ducked out into the night, running from the zombies that joined the creature at the entrance, and headed for the jeep.

———

FREYA FINALLY GAVE INTO TEMPTATION AND CALLED Erik. He agreed to meet up for breakfast, and as they sat across from each other, he looked into her eyes and touched her hand. There was an electric shock between them. She wanted him, but her fear stopped her from pursuing anything. She let go of his embrace.

"Are you okay?" he asked, brushing her hair from her face.

Freya's cheeks burned under his touch.

"Yeah, I'm okay," she stuttered and smiled.

"I like you, Freya," he said out of nowhere. "You don't have to say anything, but I'm here in case you do."

She stared blankly at his face, struggling with her mixed feelings, not wanting to get hurt again.

"When are you leaving?" She changed the question.

"In two days, back to New York," he replied.

"I'll come with you!"

"I thought you came here to visit your uncle?" He made it sound like a question.

Freya shrugged. "I did, but I think he's ignoring me. I can't seem to get a hold of him anymore. I'm just gonna give up; he clearly doesn't want to be found."

"You should stay," Erik said. "You've come this far already."

But Freya shook her head. "I'm done looking for him. Besides, I'd rather not stay here alone. Everyone around here seems to be losing it. I can't even count how many I've had to save from getting hit by a car."

On her last day in Istanbul, Freya headed back toward her hotel after spending the morning at Erik's. Her flight was in twelve hours, and she wanted to take a warm bath before heading home. But as she arrived, she saw a man standing at the front steps of the hotel, and something about him looked familiar.

"Freya Moore?" He was a tall and chiseled man with green eyes and black hair.

"Yeah, who are you?" she asked, though she already knew the answer.

"Your uncle, or to be precise, your biological mother's brother," he replied. "Name's Richard, and it's a pleasure to meet you."

"Where were you? I've been calling you and messaging you for days!" she confronted him. "Why show up now, when I'm about to leave?"

"Well, I had my little friend look out for you. He wanted to tell you, but I made him promise not to," said Richard in an arrogant manner.

"Yeah, yeah, whatever. Are you coming in or not? Because I have a flight to catch soon," she said.

"I know. We're going back together," he replied.

"What?" Freya asked.

"Little Freya, your flight has been canceled. And you will accompany Erik and I on a private jet back home," said Richard as he followed her inside and stood at her door.

"Is there anything else you'd like to throw at me?"

"No, only that you have thirty minutes to pack," he replied while going through her snacks.

Freya huffed and threw her belongings in her bag, annoyed. Now that she had finally found what seemed to be her biological family, the man turned out to be a jerk.

"One more thing, be prepared to meet your mother... I'm taking you to her."

What? My mother died giving birth to me. Freya's whole world stopped as her hands froze on the zip of the suitcase.

CHAPTER FOURTEEN

As the sun rose above the offices of the Pyramid, Freya gazed up at the structure of steel and stone. In her right hand, she held the gun, while the security card was tucked in her left sleeve. The jeep was still running behind her as she stood in the parking lot.

Dan had left his phone in the car, so she'd been able to monitor the comings and goings of the staff inside. She also heard that Kairi had returned to her office in order to monitor the new virus. Freya found more bullets in the glove compartment, but it still didn't seem like there were enough.

The sun was rising, and the zombies were beginning to slow down. Lucky for her, it made it much easier to get inside. When she walked in, there was a distinct smell of rotten flesh and death coming toward her as she opened the double doors, but she saw nothing but smeared blood and bullet holes.

She decided against taking the elevator, not like it was working, anyway. She took the stairs, one at a time, making sure to avoid making too much noise. Her body throbbed from the night before, but the adrenaline pumping through her veins hid the pain.

She reached the row of offices where Kairi had supposedly hidden. There was an eerie silence and tension in the air. She placed a hand on the knob to Kairi's office and closed her eyes. She took a deep breath, and said a short, little prayer.

"This is for you, Dan," she whispered. "For Mom and Cyrus, and everyone hurt by the Pyramid."

Once again, she kicked in the office door with her gun held high. She waited just a fraction of a second to make sure she could see Kairi clearly.

"This time, I will not miss," she cried.

But the room was empty.

She lowered the gun when something hit her in the neck. She touched the dart that had embedded in her body, and as her vision went blurry, she could see Kairi step out from the shadow.

"Stupid little girl," Kairi said. "You are so predictable. Come into my lair, said the spider to the fly."

Freya's vision failed as she fell to the floor, dropping the gun at the same time.

———

"MOM, WHY DID YOU CALL ME IN HERE?" NICK ASKED when he made his way around the living room.

"I have a surprise for you. Have a seat. Where's Kairi?" his mother asked.

Although she was in her late forties, she was still as beautiful as the morning sun.

"Really? You still expect her to show up? After everything you've done? Remarrying after Dad died? You know she still hasn't forgiven you for it, and there's no way she's coming." Nick grabbed a glass of water and sat down.

His mother, Danielle Picardo, was an active member of Cabal. She joined at the age of seventeen, fell in love, and married Ezra Harridan, CEO of Cabal. Ezra was twenty at the time, the heir of his father's company. Ezra taught Danielle how to stand up for herself and get ahead in the company. In the midst of all this, they found comfort within each other.

Ezra was like an ocean, but Danielle was a storm. Her impulsivity was perfectly balanced out by his calmness. A few years after their marriage, they had twins: Kairi and Nick.

However, tragedy stuck when Ezra went to war and never returned. He died fighting for Cabal. No one knew how or what happened. His children were four years old at the time, and Danielle was only twenty-three. She lost herself, her happiness, her purpose in life. She became a passive member of Cabal and moved with her children to South Dakota for a few years.

There, she met an ex-member of Cabal, Kevin Moore. And for the sake of her children, she remarried and had a daughter with him, Freya. However, Danielle was so ashamed by this that she sent Nick and Kairi to live with their grandmother, and Freya to live with her sister, a sin she could never forgive herself for. She never had a great relationship with her sister, and hadn't really spoken to her much, and it'd been only years later that she found out of her sister's passing, and little Freya falling prey to the system. She had been thrown from foster home to foster home, but by the time Danielle found out about her whereabouts, she was already with a good family, and Danielle didn't know what else to do.

She'd wanted to explain herself over the years, but never found the courage to do so, with numbness rooting in her. But now... now it was time. She might be running out of time.

"I have something very important to tell you, and someone I want you to meet," Danielle announced.

"Aw, come on, Mom. Not another date. How many times do I have to tell you? I'm not ready to find love again." Nick slumped on the couch and grabbed the remote.

"It's not that." She sighed and looked down at her hands. "Nick... I've been having a few tests done lately, and there's... there's something not quite right with my health. And I've been keeping a secret from you for too many years. I need you to know in case I forget..."

"What are you talking about, Mom? You're not making sense," Nick interjected.

Danielle shook her head. "It doesn't matter, I don't matter, but you need to know... You have a half-sister, Nick."

Nick dropped the remote. "Excuse me?"

"When I remarried, Kevin and I had a daughter. But I was so ashamed of her that I sent her to live with my sister, who then passed away. The girl ended up in foster care, and I lost track of her for a while. Her name is Freya..." She sat down beside him. "Here's her picture." Danielle glowed as she talked about her daughter with Kevin, pure innocence in her voice as she showed a picture of a younger Freya, only a teen. "She'll be here any minute now." She checked her watch and smoothed out her dress.

When they both walked out onto the front porch, a black limo pulled into their driveway. Richard came out first.

"Richard!" Danielle greeted her brother with a hug. "How was the trip?"

"Same as usual. Cabal had me running all over the place. I'm just glad I had Erik here to keep our Freya company." He stepped aside as Erik got out of the limo.

"Name's Erik. It's nice to meet you!" Erik bowed and shook Danielle's hand. They all exchanged a few words while Danielle nervously played with her hands.

"Well, where is my little Freya?" she asked after a moment. The girl wasn't a girl anymore, but it was hard to think of her as anything but.

"She's right here. Freya, can you come out, please?" Richard called out.

When no one came out, Richard called out her name again. "Freya! This is very disrespectful. Please come out right now and meet your mother!"

"Um, sir," Erik said as he poked his head inside the limo. "She's gone..."

"What?!" Richard looked inside the limo. It was empty, the door on the other side open, and the expanse of forest around their property now seemed more like a trap rather than protection.

She's gone?

———

WHEN FREYA CAME TO, HER HEAD ACHED AS A BRIGHT light shone in her eyes. She tried to move, but found that she was strapped down to a gurney, and all she could move was her head.

"Where the hell am I?" she croaked as she fought the restraints.

"My lab," Kairi said casually, coming into view.

Another figure dressed in a white robe joined her. He was balding, with gray hair like a crown around his dome. In his hand, he held a syringe filled with a neon green liquid.

"What is that? What are you doing?" Freya winced at the needle glistening in the light.

"Well, Freya," Kairi said softly. "You have become quite the thorn in my side. It's time I get rid of you once and for all! And lucky for you, I've been looking for more people to join my little experiment."

"Don't," Freya pleaded.

"But then again, it's not like you're the first." Kairi smiled again. "Have you ever stopped to wonder what happened to your brother, Cyrus? How long has it been since the last time you saw him?"

Freya's heart stopped. *Cyrus.* The last thing she could remember was leaving him to fend for himself after he kept pushing her away for his phone. And then, suddenly... He'd just vanished, gone. She'd assumed he just didn't want to be found. That he was back into drugs, maybe hiding out in some den or something. But now... now...

"What did you do to him?" Freya demanded.

Kairi cackled. "Why don't you just ask him yourself?" She pushed a button, and a door flew open, revealing the monstrous creature bound in cuffs and chains. Kairi had been paying close attention to Freya for a while, not trusting her with all the snooping around she was doing, and when she'd found out that she had a brother who was deeply involved with the Pyramid, it had been too perfect to ignore.

"No," Freya whispered. "You can't do this!" she shouted to Kairi.

"Watch me." Kairi threw an evil grin. She looked over at the man in the white coat and nodded. Freya squirmed as she felt the needle enter her arm, cold liquid flowing through her veins.

Several hours later, Freya woke up as the anesthesia slowly wore off. Her head felt dizzy, but she moved to her side, cradling her legs. As she lied there, tears slowly streaming down her face, she realized that she could move. She was no longer strapped to the gurney. She stopped her sobbing and turned onto her back. The bright light still shone on her, and she had an IV stuck in her arm. A tube ran from the needle stuck in her to a now empty bag hanging from a moveable iron rod.

"Freya?"

She looked around. The small room was completely empty, except for a small table with surgical tools... and Nick.

I'm still me, Freya thought. *The virus didn't infect me?*

"Freya, are you okay? What happened?" Nick asked.

Freya shook her head, unsure of what to say or do. She was about to attack Nick, but the softness in his eyes made her think twice. *Which side is he on?*

"What are you doing here?" Freya asked instead, holding still for now.

"I heard Kairi was up to something, and I came to

check... I didn't think... I didn't expect her to... Does she know who you are?"

"Who I am? What are you talking about?"

Nick opened his mouth, but then closed it sharply as they heard footsteps in the hall. Nick motioned to her to close her eyes, and he rushed to a side door, disappearing behind it.

One of the doors opened, and Freya closed her eyes and pretended to sleep as Kairi and the doctor walked into the room.

"So, according to our calculations," Kairi began, "based upon the earlier experiment we did, the process should be done."

"She'll soon be just like her brother," the doctor interjected.

"Indeed, Dr Wells," Kairi replied. "She will be the second subject, and if this goes well, we can get ready to release it worldwide."

They came closer to look at her.

"Freya," Wells said softly. "Time to wake up."

In one swift motion, Freya yanked the needle from her arm and stabbed it deep into the neck of the doctor and slashed down. He yelped as blood streamed from the gash in his neck.

"Stop it," Kairi commanded, but Freya simply kicked her in the chest.

"Your damn virus has no effect on me," Freya screamed and climbed off the gurney.

She walked toward Kairi, who scooted backwards toward the other door.

"I am impressed, Freya." Kairi laughed. "Your will to bring us down has trumped the virus, and here you are, stronger than ever. I would like to thank you for this, because now I know that we have to work on a new algorithm. One that can't be overcome."

"That will never happen." Freya stood tall. "Because you won't make it out of here alive."

She took another step, but Kairi grabbed the handle to the door and opened it. As it swung open, she could see the hulking shape of what used to be her brother, Cyrus. It stumbled forward with heavy steps.

"Kill her," Kairi said and pointed to Freya.

The creature ambled forward, arms raised, and let out a deafening snarl. Kairi ducked out of the room as soon as Cyrus came at Freya. Freya dodged and could feel the air move as the dirty hands missed her by an inch.

"Cyrus," she cried. "Stop it. It's me, Freya."

"Freya, careful!" Nick yelled from somewhere inside the room.

The creature ignored the plea and swatted at her. This time, it didn't miss and sent Freya flying across the room. When her world stopped spinning, she watched in fear as Cyrus came at her.

"Cyrus, stop! I don't want to hurt you!" Freya screamed, but with no luck. In a second, Nick stood in front of her, arms raised to the sides.

"Kairi has taken everything from me," Nick said, "she won't take you, too!"

Freya struggled to understand what Nick was talking about, but there wasn't much time to ask as Cyrus threw another fist, this time, sending Nick against the gurney, and then Freya the other way. The fall split her lip, and she could taste the blood pouring down. Her legs were wobbly, but she managed to support herself with the IV stand close by.

"Nick, are you okay?" she yelled. Nick opened one eye, looking worse than she did.

Cyrus took a step toward her, and Nick yelled with the little air left inside his lungs. Kairi had killed Fatimah, and then created the virus that infected Clarissa. Nick had spent the last few hours with the woman he loved, watching her worsen second by second, until she could speak no more. Until all she wanted was to eat him alive. And he had to do what was needed in order to survive. In order to remain strong enough to avenge both their deaths. He wasn't about to let the same happen to Freya. He remembered now. Freya. Who she was. His little sister.

"Hey, scumbag!" he yelled at the monster, who turned to him with a snarl. Nick took the gun he'd been hiding in his belt and aimed it at the creature's chest. As he fired, the noise echoed in the small lab, and the creature fell forward... or so he thought. Everything moved in slow motion as the beast pounced at him, clearly weakened, but not enough. The massive fist collided with Nick's chest, stealing the remaining air out of his lungs, and the room spun, and then went dark.

"Don't make me do this," Freya yelled.

The creature howled with rage and turned to her. She was holding the IV stand like a bat, her legs ready to leap. The creature advanced toward her, slipped on the blood from Dr. Wells that covered the floor, and crashed hard onto the tile, head first. Freya saw her opportunity, held on strongly to the IV stand with both hands, and aimed it at Cyrus' head.

She closed her eyes as the point of it pierced his skull and pinned him to the floor. With all her weight, she leaned on the stand, waiting for the shaking of her brother's body to subside. She breathed heavily as blood from her face intermingled with her tears, and then she ran toward Nick, his body unconscious on the floor.

"Nick, Nick, are you okay?"

She slapped his cheek, and only one of his eyes opened; the other too bruised to move.

"I-I..." A trickle of blood came down the side of his mouth, and then Nick coughed a few times, his eyes losing focus, and blood still coming out from between his lips.

"Nick, don't do this to me, come on! Breath!"

"You... you should... know..." Nick's words barely made it out of his lips, and he lifted one hand to cup Freya's cheek.

Freya's heart was going crazy as Nick tried to get a few more words out, but instead, coughed some more blood, and then... nothing. His chest didn't rise or fall, and his opened eyes didn't seem to see her anymore.

"Nick? Nick... come back! What should I know? Nick?"

But no matter how much Freya tried to bring him back, Nick didn't reply, his ribs broken inside his chest, his lungs punctured, and his heart no longer beating.

CHAPTER FIFTEEN

The Pyramid continued to gain more and more users from around the world, news of what was happening in the United States foreign to the rest of them. The reach had extended to almost every sector of civilization, to the entirety of the entertainment industry. Owners of large businesses mass promoted the Pyramid, and this directly gave Cabal the biggest breakthrough in history.

Sitting in front of her painting in her lounge, Kairi rested her head on her hand and placed her elbow on the arm of the sofa. She pondered for a while, when it occurred to her, a way to extend the reach of the Pyramid even further, and take its poison to yet another level. Especially with the new and improved viral formula they were going to manufacture.

Kairi called another emergency meeting at dawn. She prepared herself; she loved the feeling of preparing to present her ideas. She took a bath and donned a black suit with a coat and scarf above. She stood in front of the mirror, and said to herself, "You're a bad girl, Kairi, but I love you, nonetheless."

Kairi arrived at the ground floor of her building. She called Silvia over and told her, in a careful tone, to keep an eye out for any intruders who tried to break in. Kairi knew she wasn't the most popular person, and she certainly didn't need any rioters breaking into her home.

In the conference hall, a journalist asked Kairi a question.

"Kairi, could it be that the Pyramid is trying to become the center of the entire digital media? And from there, it's aiming at world domination, or some form of it?"

The question was a shock, dropped at the perfect moment. A telecast that was being broadcasted worldwide; a question had finally been raised directly about the nature of her work and her goals. She quickly collected herself, blinked her eyes, and smiled. Looking at the journalist, she took a sip of water from her glass and said, "Well, of course, my goal, or rather the Pyramid's goal, is world domination, but it doesn't resemble Stalin's view. We want to dominate the world with peace, where every one of the humans has equal opportunities. A world where no child will be disappointed by their dream, and no woman or man shall have to face a night with unsatisfied hunger. And I definitely couldn't have done it alone; even the janitors and cleaners working in our buildings all over the world are worthy of praise for being a part of this beautiful journey."

She chose her words carefully, rendering praises and applause from the press while the people watched. But deep inside, she had a question, a question that bothered her every time.

Kairi sent one of her interrogators to question the journalist about the reason for such a political question. It wasn't a smart move; the question could have been nothing but a guess or an attempt by the person to ask something different. Whatever it may be, Kairi was desperate; the uncontrollable release of the virus had made her paranoid as she failed to accept the mere reality.

The men contacted her and told her that she indeed had a mole in Cabal. Without thinking or pondering, Kairi screamed over her phone to her assistant to locate and bring the two men, Flint and Atlas, to her mansion the same evening as they had both always rejected her ideas. One of them had to be the one to blame.

Even though they were on the same societal level as her, Kairi enforced her power on them. She became more unstable than before. Before ending the call, she ordered the interrogators to murder the journalist and bury his body in an undisclosed location.

———

LATER THAT EVENING, THE TWO GENTLEMEN ARRIVED. They were startled and confused as to what could have caused such a sudden summon.

Kairi prepared a room for them in the lower ground lab. She placed the artifact on the table, linked to two watches and a computer. Both men were told to wear the watches without much information, and as they fell into a state of confusion and disarray, they could not resist. As soon as they wore the watches, Kairi passed a smirk and loosened her nerves.

She inched toward them and sat on a chair across from them. She pressed record on the tape recorder and started interrogating. She warned them that the watch was only one step away from injecting them with the virus. Every lie would be detected with unfriendly consequences. She imbued them with the truth about the artifact and the strain it possessed.

"I'll be direct, and not beat around the bush. So, tell me, which one of you released the information to the press?" Kairi asked with piercing eyes.

When no one spoke up for the next few minutes, Kairi sharply tapped the desk, which jerked the men to attention.

"I did it. I know you're going to kill me for opening up to the journalist, but I can't let you do this," Atlas cried out. "Please, Kairi, we need to stop this. You need to stop this. For me." He pleaded with a glimmer of hope in his eyes that he could play to her soft side.

Kairi stopped her tapping.

"Atlas," she whispered.

She'd always loved him. Too afraid to let her guard down to be with him, but she'd always cared for him. She had met Atlas when her father was still in charge of Cabal. She was just another wide-eyed teenager, innocent as a child, when she first met him. They spent all their time together, and in time, started falling for each other. Kairi wasn't always a cold-hearted killer. That was, until her father passed away.

She lost it after that, becoming immune to emotions

and constantly seeking revenge. Atlas tried his best to be there for her, but she eventually closed off from him also, treating him as just another employee rather than her former lover.

But she shook away the memories and powered the computer. He started crying, forcing himself off the chair, but the straps grew even tighter. Both his hands and feet were restrained. Kairi took a deep breath, looked at him with a glimpse of sadness and disappointment, and said, "I loved you, Atlas. And I thought you loved me, too. Why'd you have to go behind my back like this? Why?" muttered Kairi.

"I don't want you to lose control. That's all. You are ignoring the consequences that this will have," shouted Atlas.

"Oh, shut up. You don't know what you're talking about," snorted Kairi.

She pulled out a syringe and injected him. He closed his eyes, tears coming down his cheeks. His chest tightened with immense pressure on his heart. He wailed for breath and started suffocating. He turned blue due to the lack of oxygen. Kairi hurriedly came next to him, released the restraints, and ordered the doctor to shut down the machine. She thought it was another normal procedure; why did it get out of control?

She picked up the artifact and took it with her after ordering her guards to release Flint.

"We have to release this soon before word gets out. Use the system to hack into the Pyramid's portal and release it. NOW!" She ordered the tech in charge.

As the night fell, Freya emerged from the laboratory. She walked on unsteady feet. She walked up the staircase toward the center of the Pyramid, where she knew the artifact containing the virus must be. She was going to finish this, one way or another.

As she reached the first floor, a zombie came at her. In pure shock, she swatted at it, taking its head from its shoulders with ease.

"What? How?" she asked herself out loud.

Another ghoul came at her, and she did the same. She looked at her hands. Whatever Kairi had injected her with hadn't turned her into a monstrous creature, but it had given her superhuman powers. Now, the game was changing.

———

There were wildfires in the southern forest that took down many animals and trees. With its unstoppable intensity, it became an eternal blazing flame. No one could escape it. That was exactly how the virus spread across the world. It was encapsulating every human who held onto their phone.

Zombies continued to form. No one knew the cause of this insanity. Doctors were losing wars. Nurses lost themselves. People sat on the street, night after night, on their phone, slowly turning into one of them, but they didn't care. All they cared about was the app, scrolling and scrolling and scrolling.

Kairi returned to her office at the Pyramid headquarters. Silently, she looked at the documents scattered all over the desk. The artifacts, the algorithm, and the entire plan behind the Pyramid and the virus. She tapped the documents and walked over to the huge windows looking out over the city. Chaos reigned supreme out there. Zombies were wreaking havoc on those who hadn't yet turned. She'd hoped to feel pride at her accomplishment, but no. There was something else there. The pang of guilt ravaging her mind.

In her fury, she had released an apocalypse. She walked back to the desk and looked at the solitary syringe among the documents. She could fight it no longer. Her actions would have more dire consequences than she had hoped. Someone would have to pay the ultimate price.

———

Zombies came at her from all angles as Freya made her way into Kairi's office, but she beat them off with her new-found strength.

This time, she did not hesitate and walked right into her office. She found the woman sitting on her chair, turned away from the door.

"Kairi," she said. "It ends here and now. The virus, the app, everything."

She was only met with silence.

Freya grabbed a letter opener from the desk and walked closer. She could hear Kairi breathing heavily, raspy breaths in short spurts.

"Kairi?" She turned the chair, only to find Kairi's pale face with yellow eyes snarling at her.

An empty syringe fell to the floor.

"Damn it!" Freya cried as Kairi darted from the chair, flying at her.

On instinct, Freya met the attacker with the letter

opener, sinking it straight into the skull of the former CEO of the Pyramid.

Kairi dropped to the floor with one final groan. Freya mimicked the action and leaned over the desk. Without hesitating, she began rifling through the papers and documents.

"There must be a cure here," she said.

The more she looked through the papers and the algorithm, the more panicked she became, and soon realized why Kairi had taken the way out that she had. She sank back in the chair where Kairi had once sat. There was no cure. They never bothered to concoct one. This was supposed to mark the end of the world. There was a note that Dan was supposed to look into a possible solution, but he was gone now.

She rose from the seat and walked out of the office. What could she do now? There was nothing left.

As she headed down the stairs, she mindlessly fought off more zombies. This was going to be her reality for the foreseeable future. Maybe she could gather a cadre of friends and leave town, build a safe haven to start over.

The sun was beginning to rise as she stepped outside. The underground bunker could only be reached from the outside. She hesitated for a moment, wondering if she should head there or for the hills.

A group of zombies ambled toward her. Dead bodies laid all around, victims of the undead. Some had managed to take a few of the zombies with them, but all in all, the area was littered with death. She was ready to attack, hoping to take out as many as possible.

Then she saw him step into the light of the morning sun. Dan. He looked pale and scaly as he hobbled toward her, arms reaching as if wanting to embrace her.

"Dan," she whispered. "I failed."

She moved closer to him, looking deep into his eyes, hoping to find the man she loved behind them. She curled up to him and kissed him on his cold cheek. He paused for a moment to look down at her. She smiled and went in for a kiss.

Their lips met for a moment in a tender romantic gesture. Slowly, Dan let his teeth replace his lips, and he bit her hard, sinking his teeth into her tender flesh. Freya refused to cry, only letting it happen. Finding Dan had allowed her to understand that she didn't want to run or hide or fight anymore. She just wanted to give in.

As the sun rose over the city, a new zombie, a former warrior against the evil of social media, walked with her former lover along the street littered with corpses. A new day was breaking over the world. A world that was on the precipice of doom.

MIDNIGHT APOCALYPSE

VIOLA TEMPEST